THE RAINS OF ERIDAN

ALSO BY H. M. HOOVER

The Delikon

The Rains of Eridan

H. M. HOOVER

THE VIKING PRESS   NEW YORK

First Edition
Copyright © H. M. Hoover, 1977
All rights reserved
First published in 1977 by The Viking Press
625 Madison Avenue, New York, N.Y. 10022
Published simultaneously in Canada by
Penguin Books Canada Limited
Printed in U.S.A.
1   2   3   4   5   81   80   79   78   77

Library of Congress Cataloging in Publication Data
Hoover, H   M   The rains of Eridan.
Summary: When Eridan is researched for possible human
colonization, carnivorous cryptobiotic creatures emerge
during the rains on the planet and terrorize the scientists
of Base Three.
[1.   Science fiction]   I.   Title.
PZ7.H7705Rai   [Fic]   77–23533
ISBN 0–670–58931–4

FOR ROSIE

THE RAINS OF ERIDAN

Prologue

THERE among all possible worlds humanity could have made a fresh start. The planet was untouched and unknown. There was no sign of any previous civilization—no shards, no coins, no ruins, no remains of any technology. But the world was old beyond human comprehension.

The mountains were worn, the rivers wide and slow. The leaves on the great trees hung limp, not quite dry, brown, yet never falling.

It was an Earth-type planet. Yet it was not. The stars that lit its nights were stars Earth never knew, stars that wheeled too slowly through the darkness and sank each dawn into sienna seas.

It had beauty, that world, so much beauty. Sunsets and dawns that flamed cliffs scarlet against the brown mountains, turned billowing clouds pink. Flocks of kalpas flew like calligraphy against the yellow sky.

In the swamps great browsers moved, unaware of man, indifferent to one another. What man called birds sang no songs— not for human ears. On endless plains vast herds grazed in migrations only dimly understood.

A primitive world. So still, so patient—dreaming. Almost asleep.

It was most noticeable in the mountains, this sense of wakeful dreaming. Alien humanity felt most alien there, as if there were quiet sentinels waiting for something to awaken, something of an antiquity almost as old as the mountains themselves.

There was no water in the mountains, only rock and sparse grass, and small, bright-eyed, furry creatures. They never fled from humans, only watched and called to one another in flute-shrill voices that echoed through the canyons. Only when man came close enough to touch them would the little creatures move away and watch. But with the innocence of the primitive or the pure.

There were crystals in the mountains, scattered among the stones of long-dry streambeds, perhaps broken free from the vug in which they formed, or leached up from some deep volcanic tube. But they were never found *in situ,* never part of the living rock. Always free.

The humans picked them up and kept them. Naturally. For their scientific interest, for their beauty . . . and for their value. They did this out of ignorance but with no malice.

And the waiting ended.

I

SHE woke up alone, not knowing what had wakened her, but not afraid. There was nothing to fear. There was no other human for five hundred miles. No other animal here was dangerous. Lightning—she remembered lightning. The sky was clear. A few stars were still visible overhead. A dream, she decided, and turned over in the sleeping bag.

The rustle of her movement blurred a sudden foreign noise. She froze, waiting, balanced uncomfortably on her right hip. A stone dug into her arm. Then came a series of ringing thuds, like footsteps descending metal stairs. The hair stood up on her arms, and her heart rhythm tripled.

The woman was camping in the remains of a ruined cave.

Roof fallen open to the sky, the cave was a rock pocket in the mountain's skirt, unique only in that its floor was carpeted with grass because of a spring cupped under the overhang. A waist-high wall of rock blocked the view in all directions except west.

"Keep walking!" a voice called in the valley below. "Walking! Walking!" the rocks echoed. As quietly as she could, she eased open the sleeping bag and crawled to look over the wall.

The sky in the east was turning yellow. It was still dark in the valley. She could hear the stone-scuff of people moving and what sounded like a woman's urgent whisper, but she could see no one. Dry air and mountains do strange things with sound and with imagination. She picked up her camera, switched it to night lens, and aimed at the sound. The footsteps became faster and broke into a run.

A pencil-thin light beam drew a straight blue-white line across the darkness. Once, twice, and twice more. A light so bright that, when it was gone, linear images ghosted her retinas. She heard something soft and heavy fall, rocks chinked together, then silence.

The silence was broken by a vot calling its constant question. Its cohorts, disturbed now, echoed, "Vot? Vot?" from their burrows, sounding like a volley of popping champagne corks. She imagined them, alarmed, soft and furry, big eyes shining in the dark, and felt protective of them.

The alien whine of an electric motor stilled the vots. Looking toward the source of sound, she saw for the first time the faint outline of an aircraft parked on the valley floor. Its running lights were off. There came the cushioned thud of a hatch closing.

The motor's whine increased in pitch. The craft lifted slowly, like a great black ray from the ocean floor, until it hovered above the surrounding mountains, then suddenly shot away to the north. A wave of cold wind washed back across the peaks and died away. Silence returned. In the stillness the vots hesitantly began to question the happening. No more than five minutes had passed since she had been awakened.

All her awareness had been focused on listening and seeing. Her body, crouched in an awkward position, began to tremble. With effort she stood erect, then abruptly sat down on the sleeping bag, knees shaking. Seeing the craft had made her forget. She had been witness to murder.

A long, high-pitched wail of human pain arched up from the valley. It echoed to diminishing whispers of "Oh's." The woman caught her breath with fear. The vots stopped calling, too. The cry was not repeated. But someone was still alive down there, probably hurt. The woman pulled on a pair of boots, felt among her possessions for her medikit, and then, as an afterthought, her handgun and torch.

There was a natural path from her camping spot, a narrow ledge that wound around until it met another outcropping that formed a switchback down to the sloping valley wall. It was easy going, just light enough now to see the edge. Far-distant mountains were glowing red. High clouds caught the sunlight with orange. Halfway down the second ledge she stopped.

The craft had landed over there. In daylight weight marks would be visible. From the sounds, the victims had walked west up the slope, this way. As she stood there in the stillness of half-light, it seemed to her that she was being watched. Strain as she might, she could see no one. She kept weapon in hand as she walked on, soft boots whispering on the stone.

The torchlight found them about fifty feet down from the ledge. The man lay eagle-spread, eyes open to the sky; the woman on her side, one hand beneath her cheek as if she had curled awkwardly into sleep over a very large boulder.

An inch-wide white streak slashed across the woman's black hair. She knelt and gently touched it. The ashes powdered beneath her finger, and she saw the laser's stripe continued down across the left side like a lethal brand. In this light she couldn't see where the man had been hit. She leaned across and put her fingers on his brown wrist. As she did so, someone whispered, "You can't help them. They're dead."

II

THE whisper came from nowhere. The woman, hearing it, did not move, but her eyes searched the shadows around her. And saw nothing. It was the whisper of a child or young woman; she wasn't sure which. It was the voice that had cried out in pain.

"Are you hurt?"

Silence.

"Where are you? Are you . . . alone?"

After a moment she thought she could hear crying. But then she wasn't sure. But if it was a child, a child who had witnessed this . . . "I won't hurt you. My name is Dr. Leslie. Theodora Leslie . . . I'm a biologist. I'm out here on a research project . . . I've been alone out here for a month. . . ."

No response. Even the vots remained silent. Dr. Leslie eased her weight from one ankle to the other, but carefully, as a stalking animal would move in order to keep from alarming its prey. The mountain behind them was a massive blackness against the morning, the valley still in its shadow.

"If you won't tell me who you are, perhaps I can find out for myself," the woman said. As gently as possible she searched the victims' pockets for identification. There was none. Nor did they wear any jewelry or sign of class or rank. The only thing on each body was their white coverall suits. The watcher would be unarmed.

There was no point in wasting any more time. "Whoever you are, you are being foolish. If you've been shot too, you should have medical attention now before the pain becomes too severe. If you're frightened . . . well, you are frightening me. I'm going back to the camp and signal the research base."

"Don't! They'll know you saw them!"

Theo swung the light toward the cry. From behind a slab of sandstone a figure in green emerged, hesitated, and then came slowly toward her in the cone of light. It was a half-grown girl in what seemed to be green pajamas.

"If you tell them, they'll just come back and kill us too."

"Who will?"

"They will. They've been fighting. Some people were killed before. . . ." She looked down and saw the bodies and fell silent.

Theo quickly moved the light away and chided herself for her thoughtlessness. If this was their child . . . but whose child? She knew they were from the administration base. She had recognized the Executive Commander's aircraft. "Let's go up to my

camp. We can talk up there. You're not wounded, are you?"
She crossed the boulders to where the stricken child stood and
was going to put her arm around the girl to comfort her. But
that seemed condescending. So instead she held out her hand and
said, "Come. It's this way."

The girl ignored the hand. "I'll follow you," she said.

It was almost daylight by the time they reached the little camp.
Theo found the sight of it oddly reassuring, as if she had been
away a long time and was glad to return safely home to familiar
household objects. To achieve some added sense of normality
she flicked on the little camp stove and set a pan of water on to
boil for coffee.

The child hung behind and watched, obviously not sure trust
was in order. Theo could understand that.

"You can sit on my sleeping bag if you like," she said, "and
maybe you could tell me your name?"

"Karen Orlov." The child looked as if this name should be
instantly familiar.

Theo sat down. Simon and Elizabeth Orlov were second in
rank only to the Expedition Commander. Karen's statement that
there was fighting now took on a new meaning. "It must be
mutiny. Who is fighting whom? Why?"

Karen shrugged. "I'm not sure. It started last week. The Commander tried to stop it. He started curfews and searching people
for weapons. . . . I think he's dead too by now. . . ."

"What started the trouble?"

"Some of them want to go home—or anyplace. Just to get
away. The others—"

"Away from what?" Theo interrupted.

"From being afraid."

"What are they afraid of?"

"Just being here, I guess. I don't know." Karen stared off into the dawn. "It's as if they all got sick with fear. It starts with them not wanting to get out of bed in the morning . . . they just want to lie curled up under their covers. . . ."

"Were you afraid—before last night—or before the fighting started?"

"No. But I never told anybody. My parents were afraid, too. I didn't want anybody to think—are you afraid?"

"No," said Theo. "Not like that."

And the girl suddenly rewarded her with a slight smile and nodded. "I guess you couldn't be too scared. Not and be here alone. Why are you?"

"Because the same phenomenon is affecting all three of our bases. As a biologist, I'm trying to find out if there is any living creature here that is fear-inducing to humans."

"Is there?"

"Only other humans."

That remark seemed to depress both of them. Theo put powdered coffee in the pot and recalled that she had only one cup. But then she hadn't expected guests. She dug a specimen jar out of her pack. It would do nicely. She gave the girl a cup of coffee that was half milk liberally sweetened and absent-mindedly drank her own coffee black while she prepared breakfast for two. It was a bit confusing, having to consider a second person's needs after being alone for a month, she explained. The breakfast was hardly gourmet stuff.

(10)

It was hard for her to keep her mind on cooking. The events of the past hour all got jumbled with one big question—what was she going to do?

To gain perspective, she forced herself to consider matters logically. She was officially an employee of the Aurora Corporation, which was a consortium of five major financial interests: Intergalactic Corporation of the Americas; Lunar Ltd.; Space Enterprises of Palus; Ringworld I; and Big Wheel Ventures, representing the Earth's moon and colonial corporations from the L_1, L_3, and L_5 regions respectively. Run on a paramilitary basis, the Aurora Corporation researched worlds with a view to human colonialization and development of all profits those worlds might offer. There was nothing to reassure her there.

On the world they named Eridan, the Corporation had established three bases along the coast of the planet's ocean: Base One, the administration and living colony research center; Base Two, for agricultural research; and Base Three, the science base to which she herself was attached.

An average distance of three hundred miles separated one base from the next, that distance between them intended as a contamination barrier. But now the same problem affected all bases, this strange fear that had threatened to abort the entire expedition when she first came out here. Obviously that had changed only for the worse.

Discipline, morale, and tranquilizers had been keeping order at Base Three, but then, she reminded herself, she had been out here a month. What could have happened in her absence? She didn't know. Perhaps the madness of fear had created mutiny and murder there, too? Perhaps Base One personnel had taken over. Perhaps she was to be left alone out here with this child. . . . "You would survive," some still center of her mind assured her.

And she would. She was dark-haired and slender, but her walk gave the impression that she felt at home on almost any world. Although by Earth's time she was young, she had seen worlds so strange and creatures so bizarre that they shocked human sensibilities. Now nothing perceived was quite alien to her green eyes, and while much delighted her, few things frightened or even surprised her. She was in her own way rather beautiful.

She decided they would have to leave here, get at least forty miles away before she could safely signal for help. Since she did not know who was now in charge of the Expedition and of her base, it would not be wise to let it immediately be known that she had been a witness to murder. Or to be found in the place where that murder had occurred. She could always say she had found the Orlov child wandering in the mountains, which was unlikely, but then meeting her on an expedition was also.

Karen was eating her hot protein cereal like a good child. She obviously did not enjoy it, but she was far too polite to say so. Theo tasted hers. It was awful. She'd forgotten to salt it. "Why didn't you tell me?" she asked, handing the salt to the girl.

"I thought maybe that was how you always cooked," said Karen. "I didn't want to hurt your feelings."

Theo grinned. The kid had character.

She was also too calm for her own good.

"I'll mix you some powdered juice. You'll like that better."

"I'm not hungry."

"It'll be small. I think you need a little."

(12)

Karen made a face when she tasted the stuff and then drank it as quickly as possible, politely. It was bitter. When she had swallowed the last of it she set the cup down. "You put a drug in there, didn't you?"

"Yes. With any luck you will soon go to sleep for a few hours."

The girl eyed Theo for a moment, as if calculating her own helplessness against this unknown person. "O.K.," she said, "it doesn't really make much difference now anyhow. Nothing will have changed when I wake up."

"Perhaps not," admitted Theo, a bit shaken by this stark attitude, "but you'll be rested. And maybe things won't look quite so bleak."

Karen made no answer but stretched out on the sleeping bag and turned her face toward the wall.

III

THEO buried the dead alone. Using a small folding shovel, it took her most of the day. To find a sandy spot where she could dig was a problem among these rocks. Before moving the bodies, she photographed them as they lay. Sometime, somehow, someone would come to trial for these deaths. She had never realized how much work it was to bury a body. Hard manual labor—without counting the emotional cost.

By the time she had finished stacking the small cairn of rocks above the grave, she was totally exhausted and it seemed a long, long way back up the mountain to her camp.

The child was still asleep when she got there. She noted that the effect of the sedative in the fruit juice had worn off; the sleep was normal, the jaws no longer clenched; respiration was deep and slow. She studied the face; even in sleep it lacked the innocence she somehow expected in a child. It was a good face—high brow and cheekbones, the small nose almost elegant, the mouth wide and well shaped—and she wondered what life would do to it. If life had a chance to do anything. Well, it would if she could help it. Like it or not, that life depended on her now. That thought gave her the necessary energy to go take a bath in the pool.

It was a bath hurried by an unexpected shyness on her part. After a month alone, she wasn't sure she liked the idea of a stranger seeing her naked.

She was fixing supper when she became aware that the other mind was awake. Glancing away from stirring the freeze-dried stew, she saw those dark eyes watching her. She smiled a greeting but said nothing. Neither did the child. The girl lay and watched the pellets that would become rolls plunked into hot water to rise, the vitamin juice being mixed, the coffee powder measured into one cup, milk into another.

"My parents never cooked," Karen said unexpectedly. It was a statement, not boasting. "If we didn't have autoservers, someone else did it for them."

"Oh."

Silence resumed, then: "I woke up for a while this afternoon." Their eyes met, the child's tear-bright, the woman's questioning. "I . . . saw you down there. I wanted to come help—"

When she saw the child's chin quiver, Theo interrupted. "That's O.K. Sleeping was the best help you could give me. I want you well, not exhausted. Would you like to join me for dinner? I'll show you my bathroom, and you can wash up in the pool."

After she'd led Karen downhill to the sanitation pit, she came back to her meal preparations. It seemed odd having this child in her care, especially since she'd been responsible only for herself all her life. And what a child. There was a very good possibility that admitting the child existed would insure the prompt death of them both. Without knowing who or what was behind the mutiny, she had no way of knowing whom to trust.

The scientific division of the Corporation had long been charged with social and intellectual elitism by the administrative and service people. If Base One was paranoid enough to kill the Orlovs, perhaps Base Three was now "The Enemy." The Agri-group had always ignored the whole issue of rank and degrees, seemingly content. Theo avoided all cliques and power factions. Politics and swollen egos had no interest for her. Better to speculate on the diversity of gliding reptiles on the planet Tanin or the creatures in that ammonia bath of Little Venus. So long as she could study and catalogue her beloved "animals," the human animal had relatively little interest for her. Nor did she like most humans much. They were an aggressive, quarrelsome lot and notoriously neurotic in their breeding habits.

It was almost dusk when they finished their largely silent meal. Theo had gotten out of the habit of casual chatter, and Karen was too busy eating to talk. She seemed to enjoy this meal. The setting sun threw distant buttes and mesas into orange relief and shaded the lowlands with blues. In the south the distant triple moons were rising, gold in the sun's light.

(16)

"What are we going to do now?" Karen asked.

"I don't know yet. I don't know what's behind . . . your being here. Do you? Could you bear to tell me what happened? How you got here?"

The black eyes looked at Theo, and then after a moment Theo saw their sharp focus blur and knew Karen wasn't seeing her any more but something from before.

"I was asleep. Someone yelled. It woke me up, and then the light came on and there were three men in my compartment. They told me to get up."

"Who were they?"

She shrugged. "Officers—they wore stretch net over their faces. They wore service uniforms. I asked what was wrong. Nobody said anything. I told them to get out. When they didn't, I rang for the guard. They yanked me out of bed by my arm." She flexed her left shoulder. "It still hurts."

"And then?"

"They took us to the landing pad and brought us out here."

"Was there any fighting in the camp?"

Karen shook her head. "It was quiet."

Theo considered this. Service uniforms could mean they were service personnel. Or they were from another faction and pretending to be service personnel. Whoever landed here in the dark had been an excellent pilot—hardly a service skill. No, she decided, it definitely would not be wise to be rescued from this spot. In fact, it might not be wise to be rescued at all. But that couldn't be avoided. She had enough food for herself for two more months. Or for one month with her guest, unless she lived

(17)

off the land. But with her aversion to killing, that would be very traumatic—and pointless. They would have to go back sometime.

They would move on in the morning, heading toward a water source. Like any disciplined researcher, she kept careful notes. She recorded the day's happenings as a unit to themselves.

IV

For the second morning in a row, Theodora Leslie was awakened before dawn. But this time she knew what had wakened her. She was freezing. In a moment of what now seemed pure madness the night before, she had grandly told Karen, "You take the sleeping bag. The survival roll will be fine for me."

She had lied. There was nothing fine about the survival roll. She got up feeling as if she were one hundred and five and suffering from space lag. After stumbling to her bathroom, she came back and brushed her teeth. The water in the pool was very cold.

"What's that funny noise?" Karen's frightened whisper startled her. She listened and felt a blush warm her face.

(19)

"It's-s-s my-my t-t-teeth."

"What's wrong?"

"N-n-nothing. I—do-do this every m-morning."

"What for?" And when no answer came, "Are you cold?"

"Oh, no," Theo said quickly and tried to stop the noise. "I'm sorry I wo-woke you."

There was no answer, and she decided the girl had gone back to sleep, which was a relief. She was very much aware of this presence of a second mind out here, more so than in normal circumstances. "I could become a hermit," she thought, "especially at five a.m." She put on water, flicked on the fuel cell, and then sat staring at the last of the stars. It was hard to believe yesterday had really happened.

"Why do you lie to me?"

"What?" The question was so unexpected that her voice was loud.

"Vot?" echoed a nearby rock dweller.

"Vot!" answered another.

"Vot vot?" said a third.

"Why do you lie to me? My mother always said people only lie to inferiors. You lied about the sleeping bag. You knew you wouldn't be comfortable outside it. And you are still cold. Do you think I'm your inferior?"

Theodora Leslie sighed. She did not like having her motives questioned at five a.m., especially if the accuser was correct and almost young enough to be her own child.

"No. I don't think you're inferior."

"Then why do you do it?"

"Well—because you and I are strangers. I wanted you to be

comfortable—and I didn't think you'd like to sleep so close to a total stranger. If we shared the sleeping bag . . ."

"Are you very shy?"

"No. I don't think so. I . . ." She paused. "Yes, I am."

"Me too. But we don't have much choice. For now anyhow. Want to crawl in and get warm?" Karen moved over in the sleeping bag.

"No. I'm awake now."

"Me too. What are we going to do today?"

"Get as far from here as possible."

"I didn't know you had a flier." Her teeth gleamed in a pleased smile.

"I don't. We're going to walk."

"Oh." It was a deflated vowel.

"Or we can stay here and wait for them to find us."

Karen thought that over. "How much of this stuff do you want me to carry?"

"Not much. It's designed for me to carry alone." She didn't add that she was doubtful of Karen's ability to walk more than five miles in the playshoes she wore without developing crippling blisters. Or that the nearest water shown on her maps was at least twice that far away.

It took a couple of hours to have breakfast and pack up. She outfitted Karen in makeshift socks that were really soft stretch bags for delicate fossil specimens, her wide-brimmed rain hat, her favorite beige sweat shirt. The latter fit the smaller body like a short sloppy cuffed dress—over the stylish green pajamas in which Karen had arrived.

"That will never do," she decided as Karen looked disapprovingly down at herself. "Those green legs can be seen for miles."

"Oh," said Karen. "I thought that look on your face was just because I looked so terrible."

"Well . . . that too, if I'm going to be honest. Why don't we save the pajamas? You can wear a pair of my shorts and a belt to keep them on."

That ensemble didn't look all that much better, but at least it was better camouflage. By shortly after seven they were ready to go.

They set off down the mountain, Theo carrying the backpack. The vots discussed the departure in their limited vocabulary. Karen walked ahead, deliberately turning her face away from the rock pile that marked the grave site. Theo kept turning to look back until Karen said, "Did you forget something?"

"No."

"You act like it."

"No . . . I just hate to leave. . . ." She realized that might sound odd. "You see, that camp was special to me. I was alone there. For the first time in my life. I had thought—or was told—being all alone would be frightening—but it was marvelous! Peaceful. I loved the solitude." She stopped. "Admitting that must show some flaw in my character."

"I'm sorry," Karen said thoughtfully. "We spoiled it for you."

"Not by choice. . . ."

"It doesn't matter how things get spoiled. Once it's done, it's done. You can't ever make it right again. You have to accept it. And go on."

Theo looked at the small figure ahead of her. It trudged determinedly down the slope, skinny shoulders squared in the center of the sweat shirt's shoulders which ended halfway down her arms. Theo guessed that last stoic statement was being applied as much to Karen's own situation as to hers, and it touched her as much as seeing a wounded animal go quietly off to endure pain and healing. How proud the parents must have been of this bright child, she thought, and that led to thinking of the Orlovs.

She had tried to avoid thinking yesterday in the terrible intimacy of burying them. By virtue of their joint position on the Eridan Project and within the Aurora Corporation, she knew their academic and performance credentials were first rank. Their book, *A Comparison of Science and Civilization in the Known Worlds,* was a basic text in its field. Simon Orlov had been a biochemist and scientific historian, Elizabeth Orlov an anthropologist of nonhuman civilizations. Together they had made a formidable pair.

"Would you mind talking to me?" Karen stopped and was waiting for her to catch up. "I keep thinking of things and I —would you talk to me? Tell me about the animals you've seen. I like animals. Anything."

And so Theo told her stories of life forms on other worlds, cataloguing an exotic bestiary whose diversity made phoenix, chimera, and che'lin seem commonplace. She spoke of the Batoonese deltoid, a high-gravity planet creature whose flat bulk covers a quarter acre but whose mass seldom exceeds fifty pounds. And the Telarion mnese, "a small silicoid so heavy a human is unable to lift one. When a mnese reaches maturity, it fragments with an explosive sound and the fragments become the next generation. Rather like a mushroom shooting spores.

(23)

With creatures like this we are so ignorant we can do little more than note and observe. There isn't time enough to begin to understand them at all."

"What kind of eyes do they have?"

"What?"

"Do they have beautiful eyes?"

"Not particularly. The deltoid has light-sensitive cells—it's a lichen feeder."

"That's good. I'd feel sorry for it if it could see too well. All it gets to see is rocks. That would get boring."

"Yes," Theo said in a rather vague voice. "I never considered that aspect."

"Are you famous?" was the next question.

Theo shrugged. "Did you ever hear of me?"

"No."

"See?"

"How about other biologists?"

"Oh, they know my work. But we are a rare species, we extra-terrestrials. What reputation I might have is due primarily to others knowing less than I."

"That's O.K.," said Karen. "I like you. You have good eyes."

"Thank you." The non sequiturs were a bit startling. "I like you, too."

"Most people do . . . did."

Theo noted the past tense. "Do you think you're going to die?"

Karen shrugged but wouldn't answer.

"You're not, you know."

"You can't promise that."

"How old are you?"

"Why?"

"Because—I don't know. I haven't much experience with young people, but it seems to me . . ."

"I should pretend more that this isn't as bad as it really is? So you'd feel better? I can if you want me to. But it won't change a thing. I've been thinking, and the best thing you could do for yourself is leave me out here. Get miles away and call for help and say you saw an aircraft . . . then they could find me."

"Oh? Then tell me, if you insist on being a realist. How do you explain who buried your parents? No one will believe you did."

"Yes, they will."

Theo shook her head. "This is a waste of time. I'm not going to leave you and we both know that, so let's get on with it."

V

THEY were heading back into the mountains the way Theo had come. The route was not new to her. She had seen the entire area from ten thousand feet up on her initial reconnaissance flight. But the difference in perspective between an aerial view and a surface view is vast, and mountains seen from the south somehow look different when approached from the north. With the help of her compass she was in no danger of getting lost, but everything looked unfamiliar and she sought repeated re-assurance from her map.

They stopped to rest at midmorning, shared an energy bar and a drink from the water bag, and moved on. Karen's feet were in good shape. Theo found the backpack heavy, as she did the first morning of any hike, but all in all, things were going well.

There seemed to be an inordinate amount of vots. They perched on rocks, watched the aliens pass, and commented among themselves. They were still new to Karen, who found it hard to believe that a creature so cuddly and apparently so tame could not be picked up or even touched. But she kept trying.

"I won't hurt you," she assured them, but after a time she was grabbing for them. As she lunged, the vots leaped sideways and bounced away to safety.

"Why are they scared?" she asked. "I just want to pet them."

"Maybe they aren't scared," suggested Theo. "How would you feel if I reached over and petted you? And you had never seen me before?"

Karen looked up at her from under the hat brim. "I'd think you were obnoxious. Some grownups do that, you know. They pat you on the head and talk to you like you're a dog . . . 'Oh, what a nice girl you are. . . .'" She paused to consider a thought. "Do you think the vots are intelligent life forms?"

"Most life forms are intelligent. The fact that their intelligence differs from ours doesn't make ours superior—"

"Now you sound like my . . . someone else," interrupted Karen. "Are they highly intelligent?"

Theo didn't answer. Her attention had been attracted by something in the distance. Perhaps it was a trick of lighting or an ancient watercourse, but whatever it was, it looked like a road from here. Yet she hadn't noticed it before. Nor did it show on the map she hastily scanned.

(27)

"What is it?"

"Look down there, to the left of that mesa, above the line of pink rock. . . ."

"It's a path?"

"Looks like one."

"What kind of animal here makes a path?"

Theo shook her head. "None—that I've seen up here."

"Why do you look worried? Is something wrong?"

". . . more puzzled than worried," came the distracted answer.

It took them an hour or more to make their way down around the face of the mountain and across the slope. As the elevation dropped, the surface scar became less distinct until the out-cropping pink ridge was the only distinctive marker. At the end of the pink vein they found a large crystal. It lay beside a gray boulder as though it had just fallen there. It was almost a foot long, a deep orange bar, hexagonal, and perfectly terminated at both ends.

"Doesn't that look delicious!" murmured Theo half to herself as she ran a finger along its smoothness.

Karen gave her an approving glance. "Do you always want to taste them, too?" she asked, and when Theo nodded, Karen confessed, "I tasted one. It tastes just like a rock. And if it touches your teeth, pain goes right up your head. Like an electric shock."

Theo looked at her. "I trust your taste test was made after the lab reports were released?"

"Of course," Karen said, half irked. "Do you think I'm that dumb?"

"I don't think you're dumb at all. They are very tempting."

Karen gave her an appraising look, and an ornery smile came over her face. "You didn't wait to read the report either, did you?" she guessed. "You did what I did."

Theo's first impulse was to bluff—after all, adults should set standards—then she saw that face and admitted, "Yes, but it was a dumb thing to do." The girl nodded agreement.

One of the basic rules of expedition life was to consider all unknowns potentially lethal. The smallest carelessness could have tragic consequences.

"Shall we take the crystal with us?"

Theo shook her head. "It's too heavy. Besides, I've seen so many these past few weeks that they've become like wildflowers to me. Something pretty to look at—but what are you going to do with it if you pick it? Other than carry it around."

Karen sighed but nodded agreement and they went on. Neither noticed that the vots had made no sound while the two of them had looked at the crystal.

The stone surface ended in a mixture of rocky rubble and sand. They crossed a clay area free of large rocks and were almost beyond it when Theo stopped and looked back. "I think that's it," she said. "It doesn't look the same close up, but let's go check. Can you stand a detour?"

"Sure. I like to know where paths go," said Karen. "But if it is a path, how do we know we're going *to* and not *from?*"

"We don't."

If it was a path, it was an old and unused one. There were no large animal tracks. Here and there, where the sand was deep enough, vot prints showed. The only thing that made Theo keep walking was the odd fact that boulders edged the side of the route as though they had been pushed there. It could be an old watercourse. But water from where? The path curved around a hill and edged along the pink outcropping until it was burrowing under and the outcropping loomed clifflike.

"It's a cave!" said Karen. "Look up there ahead." She started to run toward it.

"Karen!" The sharpness in her voice surprised Theo as much as the girl. She hadn't realized how tense she had become until now. "Don't . . ." How to explain the anxiety that swept over her for a moment? "Don't run," she said with deliberate gentleness. "Wait for me."

"Why?" Karen said with a frown. "You said yourself there's nothing up here but us and the vots."

"I know. But you never know what's in a cave. There might be a drop-off just beyond the entrance—"

Karen studied the woman's face and then shook her head. "That isn't why . . ." she started to say and then stopped. "Do you have it too?" she asked. As if fear were a disease.

"I did—for a minute," admitted Theo. "It's gone now."

"The same way the rest have it?"

"No," the woman said firmly, and was telling the truth.

"Do you want to go back? Not see if there's anything there?"

"Yes," admitted Theo. "But I'm going to go look anyhow. You stay here."

"No," said Karen and came back and caught her by the left hand. "We'll go together."

No tool had shaped the cave entrance. It was an opening

(30)

perhaps twice as tall as a human and thirty feet wide, jaggedly irregular. A short tunnel opened into a larger chamber.

Theo reached back into her pack and pulled out her torch. The light revealed a sandy floor littered with sand-covered mounds of something and crystals of all sizes and colors. She flashed the light over the ceiling and walls. There were no crystals in the rock. She turned the light back to the floor.

"Are those some kind of rock?" asked Karen. The two of them stood at the end of the tunnel, their bodies casting the chamber into deeper gloom. Theo didn't answer but instead played the light over the nearest pile. It looked more like a mound of ancient plastic substance, dried and brittle, which in its decay had engulfed two perfectly matched pink crystals. She lifted off her pack and knelt beside the rubble to examine it more closely, feeling, touching, tapping. It did not ring. It went *punk.*

"Sounds like wood," said Karen. "Which is not too exciting— except how did it get in here?"

"Or even outside," Theo reminded her. "There is no other evidence of tree growth, fossil or otherwise, up here. I don't think it's wood."

She put down the torch and tried to lift the mass, only to discover that it was much larger than it seemed. The drifting sand had covered almost all of it. Without being told, Karen began to dig, pushing the sand away until she said, "I think we're standing on part of it."

Theo flashed the light over the small excavation. Karen had uncovered what appeared to be part of a branch covered with very dry bark. It was hard to see with all the dust in the air.

(31)

Something gleamed in the light, and she knelt to look more closely. Attached to the end of the stump were four long scimitar-like claws. "Jackpot!" Her voice was jubilant.

"What is it?"

"I think you have just gained textbook immortality," the biologist said, "by finding a new species."

"Yeah?" The word started as a question and ended as a hope. "Footnote stuff? Really?" Karen's face slowly lit up, and the woman saw in it the pure joy of the discoverer of great treasure—treasure only the child of science could fully appreciate. "She's a chip off her parents' block," Theo thought inelegantly but correctly.

"Really," she said. "Unless I'm wrong, of course."

"Well, let's find out!" Karen set to digging like a mole.

"Wait." Theo reached over and caught the busy hands. "Don't ever dig bare-handed when you don't know what's down there. You could cut yourself on more of those"—she pointed to the claws—"or on a crystal or— Here, let me get my trowels and brush."

"I'll help you—"

"No. I know just where I put them. And put this on." She handed her a disposable inhalator. "It's very dusty." She saw Karen grimace. "I'll wear one, too."

Karen sighed, but put the inhalator on, took the trowel Theo handed her, and set to work. Theo noted approvingly that she was careful not to chip or scratch the specimen. When Theo had placed the torch to give them maximum lighting, she joined in the digging. For more than an hour the two were totally involved and completely content, and neither said a word.

VI

SLOWLY the outline of the thing began to take shape. The creature lay on its side in the sand. Dehydration had perhaps fixed its tendency to curl in on itself even more, hugging its clawed feet like a secret tucked under its body. In its present condition it was eleven feet across and seven feet wide or tall, its bulk covered with a very hard substance. It looked alien to human eyes, but not so when compared to the other life forms of its world.

"Would you care to give me a preliminary identification of your discovery, Doctor?" Theo said as she stood up to stretch her aching muscles and look over their work.

Karen checked to see if she was being mocked, and then

grinned. "In my educated opinion, Doctor, I'd say it was a cross between an elephant and a caterpillar."

"A sound judgment," said Theo, nodding. "Although I tend to favor the caterpillar theory myself."

"Think of the moth this would be," said Karen, and in spite of herself, she shivered. "You don't think it is larval, do you?"

Theo shook her head. "No. It's a mature something. But *what* I don't know."

"It's got six legs—eight if you count those two short ones at the top with the pincers."

"It needs them for the weight and length of it. This specimen is totally desiccated, and it's still so heavy we can't move it. Think what it weighed alive."

"Which end is the head?"

"Where the short arms are, I guess. It's all curled under and so dry. I wish we had a good brush."

"I wish we could see its eyes. Then we'd know if it was gentle or not."

"Well," Theo said carefully, not wanting to crush Karen's faith in eyes as a means of character assessment, "a creature this size might be harmful to smaller creatures—without intending to be. But we'd know more if we could see its feeding apparatus. Which we can't without breaking this specimen."

"Want to? There's a lot more of 'em here."

Theo shook her head. "We don't have time. I hate to spoil it with no way to really analyze what we find now. We'll come back."

"You might," Karen said flatly, "but I won't. Even if . . . this all ends well, I won't be here. They'll send me someplace. . . ."

Theo's first impulse was to deny this. But that wasn't honest. Karen knew corporate rules regarding juveniles as well as she did. Probably better. "I hope not," she said. "I will request your presence on this expedition."

Karen didn't answer right away. She stood up, dusted herself off with vigorous swipes of her hat, wiped the sweat off her face, and pushed her hair back. Then, physically and mentally composed, she suggested, "Should we film this one and the cave floor?"

The photographs that were later to become famous were taken then. The one of Karen Orlov standing behind her discovery, holding a magic slate bearing her name and the date of discovery, the shots of the creature itself, the wide-angle shot of the chamber with its shadowed background where tiny points of light gleamed in unexpected places, the shot of Dr. Leslie and her protégée, both disheveled but happily smiling into the lens. The photos showed the cave floor strewn with crystals.

When they finally emerged from the cave into daylight again and were walking down the trail of their own footprints in the sand, Karen said, "That was very interesting."

"Oh?"

"Yes. While I was digging—that was the first time since it happened that I didn't think about my—about them. I was thinking about them all the time until then. Even when I didn't want to think any more. And then, when I started digging, I forgot . . ." She stopped and looked back at Theo. "Is that bad?"

"That you forgot?"

Karen nodded as Theo caught up and they walked together.

"No. That's healthy. That's nature's way of protecting us

(35)

against pain—letting us forget." As Theo spoke, her voice changed until it seemed she was explaining to herself. "Slowly, until finally, after a long time, we remember only that it happened and that it hurt. But the pain itself is gone. And then we can remember the good days that came before. And appreciate the new things and people that come into our lives."

While she listened, Karen's eyes searched the woman's face with a shade more understanding than Theo expected from her— or found quite comfortable. But the girl said nothing for almost a mile. Then she announced very seriously, "You know, I think I'm going to like you. I'm not sure yet because we don't really know each other. But I think so. Based on the evidence at hand."

At that last remark, Theo found it necessary to wipe dust off her mouth and chin. When she could be sure of her self-control, she replied solemnly, "I think I'm going to like you, too. Based on the evidence at hand."

"Where we're going to camp, is there enough water there to take a bath?" said Karen.

"That depends on how far we can walk. It's approximately seven miles to the nearest bath."

"How long will it take us?"

"Maybe two hours. With rest stops. Any blisters?"

"No. But I itch a lot. This dust creeps into everything."

It was almost dark when they reached the small creek, so dark in fact that they were on it before they realized it. The water moved so slowly that it made little sound in its gravelly bed. But the air became sweeter for the dampness and the scent of the dwarf flame trees growing along the creek bank.

(36)

"Do we have any soap?" Karen asked. "I'm going downstream to bathe before I do anything else."

"Good idea! Besides, it'll be too cold to run around bare in another hour. By the way, bathe with your clothes on first. That'll save you from putting on dirty garments in the morning."

Karen looked as if she didn't think much of that idea, but she didn't argue. "Can I take 'em off afterward?"

"You'd better. Otherwise we're going to have a soggy sleeping bag. I'll dig out your pajamas from the pack."

After unrolling the pack, Theo set up the stove, put water on low to heat, and soaked the packets of dry food for dinner. Then she too went to bathe. The creek water was almost tepid after its long journey in the sun and too shallow to wet her much above the ankles. Nor could she find any deeper pools. So she stripped off her clothing and washed it first, enjoying the splash and soap smell after the long dry day. Absorbed in her bath, she even forgot about Karen. Getting the suds out of her hair proved to be an awkward chore in the shallow water. It was too much bother going back to camp for a cup to pour water over her head. So she soaped all over, stretched out in the water, closed her eyes, and let the creek ripple over her long body. It was delicious, this sensation, this solitude.

While she lolled in the water, fifteen minutes or more must have passed before it occurred to her to wonder where Karen might be. She hadn't heard any downstream splashing for some time. Reluctantly she sat up. The evening air felt cool on her wet skin, and she was glad to wrap the towel around her. Once standing, she could see the black silhouette of Karen sitting on a rock hugging her knees and staring up at the sky. For some reason the girl's pose and stillness reminded her of herself at that age, and the hours spent thinking long thoughts.

She was grateful for the time to herself. She slipped into her other pair of coveralls and then hung her wet laundry on handy trees. In the hills vots called to one another, almost as if they were saying good night, she thought. It seemed a shame to turn on the camper's lamp and shut out the friendly darkness, but it was hard to prepare food without it. The protein substance called meat cakes looked almost edible as she shut them into the tiny oven and mixed the rice with mushrooms and vegetables. The fruit pudding sounded good; she mixed up a pack of that.

"We'd starve without water," Karen observed from the darkness behind her, and Theo nearly jumped. "Forgot about me, huh?" The girl grinned.

"Yes, for a little while."

"That's because I'm not a habit yet," said Karen. "I'll fix our bed."

Theo noted approvingly that the girl chose a level spot and carefully removed all rocks from the area the bag would cover. Karen disappeared into the darkness and came back with her arms full of greenery. "It's tomaro weed. Nonirritating," she announced. "Makes a soft mattress."

"Where'd you learn that?"

"Mother."

"I'm impressed."

"Yes." Karen walked off for another load. By the time the mattress was laid to her satisfaction, the food was ready. They ate as if they were starved, and by the time they'd cleaned up their dishes both were groggy with sleep. Perhaps if they had been less physically tired and relaxed, they would have been more self-conscious about the newness of their intimacy. As it was, Karen said, "I never slept with anybody before. Did you?"

"On occasion."

"It's kind of nice, huh? Warmer too. But nice to have company. Especially outdoors." She pulled up the fastener on her side of the sleeping bag. "I never slept outdoors before yesterday either. Makes you feel very small to look up and see all that starry sky way up there."

Theo adjusted the inflated pillow under her still slightly damp hair. "On Earth there was a tribe that called sleeping out like this 'sleeping at the Inn of the Sky.' "

Karen thought that over so long that Theo almost fell asleep before the girl said, "I like that—the Inn of the Sky. It makes you feel at home—as if you were part of it. . . ." She fell silent and then said, "I would like to see Earth sometime. It must be so beautiful. The blue planet . . ."

"You weren't born there?"

"Oh, no, I was born in space. Two years after my parents left Earth. I was born on the cruiser *Pegasus*. But I have Earth citizenship," she added proudly. "I can go there anytime. How about you?"

"Yes. I was born in the Smoky Mountains."

"Are they volcanic?"

"No. Just hazy."

"Oh." There was a sound of a stifled yawn and a longer silence, then, "That tribe that called this the Inn of the Sky— were they human?"

(39)

"Yes," said Theo softly. "Very human." And to herself silently added, "My child not born of Earth." Beside her she heard Karen's breathing slow and deepen into sleep. For a time she watched the meteors that occasionally streaked overhead. It was almost as soporific as the faint whisper of the creek to its gravel, or Karen's breathing. As Theo drifted off, Karen rolled over and snuggled against her, more trusting in sleep than awake.

VII

THEO woke up to the chink of the cooking pan against the
stove. The sun was just over the mountain and in her eyes.
Morning winds were blowing the trees, causing brittle twigs to
rustle. Karen sat cross-legged in front of the stove, stirring something and frowning down into the pot. A flock of curious weejees fluttered about her like gross red butterflies. One settled like a
ribbon bow on her black hair and crept forward to peer down
into the pot. Karen gave her head a quick shake and her orna-
ment staggered into the air again only to drop onto her left wrist,
where it clung with its tiny clawed feet.

"You're a pest. You know that?" she whispered to it. "You
and all your friends." The weejee regarded her comically with

its stalky eyes, and then, apparently attracted by the shine of her teeth, took wing to try to land on her mouth. Karen brushed it away hurriedly, stood and waved her arms until the whole flock decided she was a hazard and flapped off toward the creek.

"Good riddance," called Theo after them.

"I'm glad you're awake," said Karen. "This coffee is beginning to smell kind of strong."

"How long has it been boiling?"

"Only about half an hour."

"Oh." Theo felt a sudden urge to skip coffee. But Karen was already preparing a mug, carefully adding the exact amount of powdered sweetened cream that Theo always used. The woman knew she could not refuse that offering. She sat up, accepted the hot mug, and pronounced it delicious.

"It's not too strong?" Karen said anxiously.

"Perhaps a bit, but I like it. Thank you. What's for breakfast?"

"Mush. It's all ready too."

The mush was not bad, especially if one was hungry as Theo was that morning. While they ate, she outlined the day's journey on the map. They would be following the creek down out of the mountain, although to follow its exact path would be impossible since a few miles ahead it sank into a ravine worn deep into the rock and then dropped in a white ribbon down a cliff face. They would be hiking a roundabout route that would eventually bring them to camp at the pool beneath the waterfall. The creek led to the Dileep River. It was at this junction that Theo had begun her walk into solitude.

"You forgot to write your notes last night," Karen reminded her. "You do that while I clean up and pack."

(42)

Theo was going to protest and then reconsidered. If she were in Karen's place, she would want the dignity of helping. And the notes should be written while the discovery was fresh in her mind. "O.K. That sounds like a good idea." And both of them set to work. An hour later they were dressed and ready to go.

It was pleasant walking along the creek bank. Flowering trees followed the watercourse; grasses grew along its banks and out wherever enough moisture existed. Where the grass was thickest, vots had been at work, harvesting. Theo noted patches of varying lengths, from lawn-smooth to almost mature seeded stalks. The vots were good little farmers.

The flame tree flower matured into a small plumlike fruit that quickly fermented in the sun. Clouds of weejees clung to the branches of these trees, feeding, or crawled drunkenly on the ground beneath. Once Theo and Karen saw a sulfur-yellow creature, a grazer of some sort, which bounced away at the sight of them. But there was little food up here to support varied animal life.

Where the creek plunged down the ravine on its way to the waterfall, they stopped to rest. So far, the hike had been easy and they had made good time. That would end now. They stood at the edge of a high plateau, looking down.

The mountain chain lifted abruptly from the plains, buttressed by long ridges thrusting out upon the flatland. Trees climbed halfway up the ridges; above the treeline the dull reds and ochres of the mountains glowed in the sunlight. But it was the view of the seemingly endless plains below that evoked an "ohh," from Karen.

It looked like some vast zoological park that stretched from mountains to horizon, accented here and there by streambed and mesa. The predominant color was the beige of grass with accents of red rock and soil and olive-brown trees. There were herds of animals scattered over the plains. Gliders, both furred and leather-winged, floated on the updrafts that carried with them the delicately sweet scent of the grass and the endless song of insects.

Karen sat and drank it all in silently, but her face told Theo all she wished to know. It was a look of appreciation of something near to the reverence the biologist felt for this land. The face had all the benign intensity, the relaxed absorption of the religious.

Theo unhooked her pack straps and swung the pack to the ground. She searched out a couple of protein bars and handed one to Karen.

"I didn't know this was out here," the girl said after a few swallows. "So big. So . . ." She could find no words for it. "It's like we—you and I and all the Expedition—could come and go, or stay. It wouldn't really matter. . . ."

"No," agreed Theo. "It wouldn't matter at all. Not to this world. But if you and I don't start walking, we're not going to make camp until after dark. And that inconvenience matters very much to me. Eat up!"

They spent the next three hours slipping and sliding and hugging belly-tight to rock faces as they negotiated the way down off the plateau. Theo kept thinking that it wasn't hard coming up, but reminded herself that coming up she hadn't been able to see quite so clearly just how far one could fall if one slipped.

At one point she removed her backpack and lowered it by rope from one ledge down to the next, then lowered Karen the same way. There was nothing on which to anchor the rope to support her weight, so she inched her way down by precarious toeholds.

Karen seemed oblivious to the danger; she was still enthralled with the view of all the animals.

By the time they reached the treeline and could walk switchbacks at a steep downhill pace, both of them were tired. It was warmer down here, almost hot in the midafternoon sun. Sweat ran down their faces, and they stopped to rest more often. Each time they stopped, Theo checked Karen's feet for blisters. So far the specimen bags made admirable socks.

"Can you swim?" Theo asked her, and when Karen said yes, "You'll like our camp tonight then. It has a lovely deep pool."

"I would like any camp tonight," said Karen and wiped away the sweat. "I would like any camp right now. How much farther is it?"

"About three miles. Tired?"

"Not yet."

"Well, I am." And she was. She had forgotten how much energy nerve strain consumed. The events of the past few days had cost her not only extra physical effort and loss of sleep but the peace of mind found in solitude—and so quickly taken for granted.

Animals became more plentiful on the lower slopes. Wherever there was heavy vegetation, there would be a small herd of creatures scattered about, feeding or resting in the shade of trees. None showed any fear of these two strange animals walking

(45)

through their domain. Several approached to view them more closely.

"Are they hostile?" Karen said nervously as a rather sturdy-looking creature, taller than she was and rust-furred with white spots, came loping up the hill toward them.

"No. Just curious," said Theo. "The total absence of predators has made them quite secure."

"What keeps their population under control?"

"Most of them are hermaphroditic. They are born male. In an adolescent stage they mate with mature animals, females, and after mating their endocrine system stimulates their maturation. It's very efficient since it eliminates the necessity of large quantities of nonproductive feeders. Or large males hostile or indifferent to infants and therefore dangerous to them. The great swamp browsers are totally hermaphroditic and impregnate themselves. When there is a shortage of food or water, these creatures simply remain in immature form. In this stage they age very quickly and die."

"That doesn't seem quite fair," said Karen. "It's not their fault."

"Fair has nothing to do with it," said Theo. "Those are rules of this world. It's what keeps those gliders alive. They are the vultures of Eridan." The word "vulture" had no meaning for Karen, and so Theo explained it. After that Karen viewed the gliders rather skeptically, regardless of how beautifully they might soar on the winds.

Where they camped that evening, a cliff stood behind them like a curtain of red stone. From high up the cliff the creek

(46)

spilled over in a ribbon of white, dropping from ledge to ledge until it reached their tree-shaded pool below. That animals came there to drink was apparent from all the tracks and droppings in the sand and the fact that the grass was eaten short for acres around. Karen was not sure she wanted to live quite so intimately with these creatures.

"What if they step on us in the dark?" she said. "Or decide our hair is good to eat?"

"I stayed here a week," said Theo. "No one bothered me. However, if you really want it, I have a tent." She unsnapped what appeared to be the backboard of her pack, an oblong about one and a half inches thick. It flipped open and open again, revealing that it was intricately folded plastic fabric. "I never bother with this. It takes so long in the morning to get the air out of the floor. Here's the telescoping center pole." And that she pulled out of the pack's base. "You want it up?"

"Will it hold both of us?"

"It'll hold four."

"Then let's, please?"

"Watch this," said Theo. She shook the rectangle of fabric as if it were a folded sheet. It opened with a snap and billowed into form. Before it had a chance to sink to the grass she caught a strategic hold and inserted the sturdy center rod.

"O.K.," she said, handing the rod to the girl. "Hold it here with your left hand and pump with your right, like so," and she demonstrated the air pump's action. "In about five minutes you'll have a house. Oh, yes, when it's fully inflated, press this button and the rod telescopes. You'll see the socket in the floor."

(47)

The tent, when Karen was done, was a rimmed dome, its walls layers of fabric sandwiching air between, its door a flap that jutted out when inflated.

"It looks like a giant yellow balloon cut in half," said Karen as she stepped out to survey her work.

"It'll blow about like one if we don't weight it down," said Theo. "Let's get some rocks on that rim."

By the time the housekeeping chores were done, they were more than ready for a swim. They fixed dinner and ate in their pajamas. For dinnertime entertainment, they watched the animals coming to the pool and stream to drink. And the animals watched them.

Or more correctly, the animals watched the tent. Theo regretted she had never used it before. It was an excellent lure; she wasn't quite sure why. The animals would approach with great interest and then stand some distance away, eying its yellowness, occasionally making sounds to their cohorts. By sunset a great crowd had gathered.

It had all the air of an occasion. On the outer fringes of the crowd gangly bearded hexalopes forgot their elklike dignity and indulged in mad little leaps and bleatings. A creature resembling a six-legged six-toed ox with a shovel-shaped head shambled up and grunted with surprise when it saw the tent. It found Theo almost as interesting as she found it; obviously both had never seen an animal like the other. But with all the eying, sniffing, and circling, both kept their distance. Karen moved back until she was sitting beneath the door flap.

As the sun's rays slanted more and more, the shade of the tent deepened and seemed to glow with life. Noise and activity among the animals increased. They moved in closer to the object of their admiration. Three shaggy sulfur-yellow grazers crept forward until they were touching the rim with their muzzles, then curled up with little sighs of contentment and fell asleep, oddly endearing with their long black eyelashes and six folded knees.

As twilight came, the crowd began to disperse, some to graze, others to drink and bathe and settle to rest beneath the nearby trees. Out of curiosity, Theo turned on the torch and set it inside the tent to make it glow yellow again. The animals came hurrying back. It was the color . . . perhaps.

"You won't mind if we go to bed in the dark?" asked Karen. "I don't want to get too friendly with our new neighbors. They might crowd us out of bed." Theo laughed and agreed, and turned off the torch.

VIII

"WHAT is that?"

Theo was wakened from deep sleep by a frightened whisper and a hand clutching her wrist. It was pitch-dark. For a second she couldn't remember where she was or where the stars had gone. She was in a sleeping bag with a cuddling stranger. Then something brushed against the outside of the tent and she came fully awake. The squeaking sound was like that of a giant hand stroking a large balloon. She felt Karen stiffen in terror and reached over to give her a reassuring hug.

"How long has it been out there?" Theo whispered.

"I don't know. It woke me up. It was licking the roof . . ."

"Shhh . . ." Theo had a sudden uneasy impression that they

were being listened to. Other than the distinct hissing of the waterfall, it was still outside . . . except for the sound of breathing—great slow breaths. And then the thing snuffled, and her heart changed its pace. The snuffle was the deep, moist, inquiring sound of a large hunting animal, and in the darkness it seemed to come from treetop height. Noiselessly she reached for her stun-gun, just as the tent was flooded with light.

"Turn it off!" Theo sat up, half blinded, and grabbed for the torch Karen held.

"I'm scared."

"Turn it off!"

There was a startled scuffling sound, a pause, and then deep pounding shook the ground as the thing fled.

Karen let out a long sigh of relief. "The light scared it! It probably never saw a light in the dark in its whole life!"

"Turn it off!"

"What if it comes back?" said Karen, but she obeyed.

Theo did not want to frighten her more, but if that big thing came back, she didn't want them to be trapped in a flimsy tent. For the first time since she had been left alone, she felt uneasy. She blamed her unease on the tent. It shut the world out, made them alien to the night.

It was very dark outside. She could dimly make out the trees, and the white of the waterfall, the outline of the mountains. But she couldn't see any animals.

"Pass me the torch," she whispered, and when she held the cold plastic in her hands, she hesitated to turn it on for fear of what the light might reveal. But there was nothing there. In a

360-degree circle not one animal remained. Just tent, trees, and water.

Set on long beam, the light reached to the cliff face. She swept the half circle behind the tent, moving the beam slowly over the distant rocks. The eyes of a large animal caught the passing light and flashed. She moved the beam back, but whatever it had been was gone. There was a smear of wetness on the tent. Like saliva.

The grass around the tent was crushed but so thick and wiry that it held no tracks.

"There's nothing out here," she announced and turned off the light.

"Where are the other animals?"

"Gone."

"Why?"

"Probably had better things to do."

"Or they got scared off."

"Maybe."

"It's so dark," Karen complained as she crawled out.

"That's because the torch was so bright."

"No. You can't see any stars."

Theo looked skyward. Karen was right. A cloud layer shut out all the sky.

"Is it going to rain?" The excitement in Karen's voice was surprising.

"Maybe. Why? What's so special about rain?"

"Well, when you spend your life on starships you don't get to see much rain. Have you ever seen snow?"

"When I was a child."

"You're lucky," Karen said wistfully.

"Well, let's go back to sleep and maybe you'll get lucky and wake up to the sound of rain on the roof."

Neither slept much for the rest of the night. It was cloudy in the morning, but no rain had fallen. Nor was there any dew. The animals had returned. Some of them became agitated when Theo let the air out of the tent and trampled it down to fold and pack. "It's not a living thing," she kept assuring them. They didn't believe her and followed as the pair set off.

It began to rain around midmorning, a soft steady drizzle. Theo made Karen an inelegant poncho out of a plastic bag; she wore her waterproof suit, but there was nothing she could do about their footgear. By midday both had wet feet. A chilly wind began to blow, and the sound of the stream made them feel colder.

The soil, dry for so long, absorbed this gentle rain. Theo wondered if it was raining harder in the mountains behind them. There, with nothing to soak up the water, runoff would be fast. She kept a wary eye on the creek and, after an hour or so of drizzle, led them far enough away to keep it in sight but enable them to outrun it should there be a flash flood.

"You know what?" Karen said after a long, silent hike. "It's nice to read about, but walking in the rain is not too much fun."

"No," agreed Theo. She wasn't feeling communicative. The pack was beginning to rub on her wet shoulders. Her feet hurt.

She was thinking longingly of her comfortable, warm, dry carpeted quarters in the living dome of Base Three, a hot bath, a glass of wine, dinner. If she had been alone, she would have signaled the Base to come get her hours ago.

(53)

If. If there had been no fear. If Base One had not mutinied. If that aircraft had landed twenty miles north of her mountain. If she had been ignorant of all that. When had that deadly dawn been—two days ago, three? It seemed a long time past. If she had ignored Karen's fear of total mutiny and signaled immediately for help. If they had never set out walking, they wouldn't have found that cave and the odd creature . . . but maybe that would never matter now. Mud clung to her feet, and she scraped it off against a rock.

If the Expedition Commander was missing and his Vice Commanders dead, then who was in charge of the expedition? Were the Base Commanders on their own? And who had enough influence or power to lead a mutiny against an Expedition Commander . . . ? No, that didn't bear speculation. Could she and Karen survive out here in the rain, wandering aimlessly? If they . . .

It occurred to her that Karen had asked her a question. "I'm sorry, I didn't hear you."

"Do you think it's raining on . . . up where your favorite camp was?"

Theo understood the question—was it raining on the grave? "Yes," she said. "I think it's raining for hundreds of miles. We knew this world had a rainy season. We just didn't know when or how often."

When the rain had begun, the animals had responded like children to the first snowfall, running and frisking, alternately dancing stiff-legged or rolling on the ground for the sheer joy of it. But now, like Karen, they had had enough. They stood in the open, tail to the wind, head down, gathering in groups for warmth, and waiting for it to end. Gliders sat in flocks, great wings like wet leather.

But the rain did not end. It grew heavier, and by midafternoon both people were cold, wet, and exhausted. Rain in the face kept them blinking; it was difficult to breathe without choking on droplets, and the ground was turning to mud. Karen was obviously struggling, but she never complained.

"Let's look for a camping place." Theo had to speak loudly to be heard over the downpour.

"Are there any caves around here?"

There were none. They were almost down on the flatland now. There was no shelter down there but trees. And if there were lightning storms on this world, camping beneath a tree was not wise. In fact, camping at all in this rain was not wise.

She chose a spot on a rocky hollow where the ground sloped enough for runoff and the tent would sit below the highest trees and rocks. Just setting up the tent was almost all they could do in the wind. By the time it was inflated and the rim weighted down, they had lost their hats so often that their hair was as soaked as the rest of their bodies. They crawled into the shelter, dragging the pack after them, wet and bedraggled.

"Don't open the sleeping bag until the fuel cell dries this out." Theo nodded at the tent floor made wet by splashing and their own entrance. Rain was pelting down on the dome above their heads and running in twin rivulets off the open dome flap. "Just sit and listen to the rain on our roof."

"It's like sitting inside a drum," said Karen, "or a surface-to-ship shuttle on take-off. But this is the longest take-off . . ." She died away to silence and sat cross-legged, watching Theo set up the little heating unit. It wouldn't stay level, and Theo went back outside to find some flat rocks to use as a base. When she came back, she closed the tent flap.

For the next two hours they were busy with housekeeping chores. The fuel cell on high quickly made the dome cozy. A washline was strung on the dome hooks provided for that purpose and their wet clothing hung to dry. Their freeze-dried food for dinner was put in to soak. Their hair slowly dried and, in spite of the closeness and the roar of the rain on the dome, they were comfortable again.

Karen was stretched out on the floor, chin pillowed on her hands. Theo used the pack as a backrest and was writing notes of the day. For minutes they were silent, each lost in her own thoughts.

Finally Karen said, "How long will the rain last? If it's the rainy season?"

"Maybe a month. Maybe longer."

Karen's sigh couldn't be heard over the rain, but Theo saw it and waited and pretended greater attention to her notes. Karen rolled over on her back and stared up at the vibrating dome. "We can't travel in it, can we?"

"No. Not very far. Not without risking illness or accident."

"What happens if we just stay here?"

"A search party will probably come looking for me."

"Will they find you?"

"Probably not—if I don't want them to. Of course it will be dangerous flying below these clouds. If they can. Especially with no directional signal to guide them. They expect me to be up in the mountains."

Karen thought that over and sighed again. "I guess maybe you'd better let them know you're here," she said. She glanced over to get Theo's reaction to that.

"I think that would be wise," Theo said calmly. "I admire your courage."

"Don't. I'm very afraid."

"I know. That makes your decision all the more admirable."

Karen rolled over with a small groan. "Oh, Theo, what if . . ." She couldn't bring herself to finish the thought.

"If they're still fighting? If anyone tries to harm you, they'll have to dispose of me first."

Karen looked up at her, eyes big and very sober. "Please don't say that," she said. "That's what my parents said. They meant it, too."

IX

THEY waited until morning to press the panic button. It was still raining, a steady gloomy drizzle. The vegetation had grown in the night. A wiry grass fringe surrounded their tent; the trees looked less limp, and the air was full of new sounds, whether of insects or amphibious creatures the biologist could not tell. And so while she waited for the rescue ship she searched the surrounding area for specimens.

Karen stayed in the tent, wrapped in the sleeping bag and anxiety, and nothing Theo could say would ease the child's fear. Every ten minutes the reply signal gave a soft but penetrating "deeep" pulse of sound, indicating receipt of a distress call and meant to reassure. But after each "deeep," Theo felt her heart go thump and knew she, too, was afraid of what that ship might bring.

It could bring one of the pilots making a routine pickup of a scientist in the field, as she hoped it would. Or, depending on the mental state of Base Three, it could bring a friend half mad with fear, as people apparently were at Base One. Or it could bring someone from Base One, if that staff had decided to do away with all Base Commanders, in which case both she and Karen were in jeopardy. Well, she decided, she would simply have to wait and see. The rain gave her little choice.

She walked slowly in the general direction of the stream, noting there were fewer animals around this morning and wondering if they had found shelter against the rain, or were beginning to move on to warmer, drier areas. Beneath a small shrub three red weejees had fallen like discarded bow ties. She knelt and examined their gleaming wetness. They were whole, apparently dead of cold. A scavenger creature which resembled a many-legged meat pudding politely waited and watched her handling its breakfast. When she stood up to go, it sidled past her and settled over one of the bodies. With an inhalation like a small suction pump, it seemed to inflate itself, then exhaled, and moved onto the next morsel. It left behind a limp pink rag hardly noticeable in the grass.

Closer to the creek a burnt-orange creature with leathery skin was moving up away from the water, its eyes dangling shrimplike above a toady body. It moved lethargically, and every few feet it would stop to peer about anxiously and emit a cry so vibrant that its entire being shook. When Theo approached, it did not hop away but rather stiffened its six legs and scuttled past her on fleshy tiptoes. She made no attempt to pick it up with her net. Try hard as she did to remain clinical, there were simply some creatures that were repulsive to her. This was one of them.

A slow chill wind swept the leaves and ruffled the creek, causing her to look up in time to see the dark shadow of an aircraft moving south through the clouds. With the rain pelting her face, she felt like a diver watching a boat hull glide over the surface of the water. The signaling device in her pocket began to chatter a *dit-dit-dit* announcement of the craft's arrival. Her first impulse was to call Karen. She opened her mouth, then stopped. It might be wiser to see who or what had come for them. She saw the shadow turn and circle back.

It broke through the murk less than a half mile away. She realized how heavy the clouds were when she saw the craft had both running and fog lights on high beam and flashing, and they had not been visible until now. The pilot skimmed a wobbly circle over the plain, obviously looking for her as well as landing hazards. She could almost feel the pilot's relief on spotting the tent. The craft lifted and swerved toward the tent's beaconlike yellow glow, bobbed up to avoid a grove, and eased down to land. The ground squelched beneath the weight of the landing pods, and the forced air cushion sent water flying. When the power shut off, she hesitated for only a moment, took a deep breath, and said out loud, "Might as well get it over with."

It was a utility craft, a squat oval work vehicle designed to transport staff and equipment to inaccessible areas. With a whine the square hatch slid up, the landing ramp slid down. The interior was empty. Then a tall figure appeared in the opening, struggling to force its head through a slot in a waterproof poncho.

(60)

"You're shoving against an armhole," Theo called. The struggle ceased for a moment.

"What?" called a man's voice.

"That's an armhole. Your head won't fit." Apparently he had come alone.

"Ah." The limp circle of blue fabric turned on the polelike body, jumped a bit and settled down over a curly head which emerged through the proper opening. "Thank you, Dr. Leslie." He grinned down at her. "Want to come in out of the rain?"

Not until he smiled did she recognize the face beneath all that hair. When had he begun to grow a beard? And why had the Base Commander come out to pick her up? Why not one of the regular pilots? As if anticipating questions, he said, "It seemed a nice day for a ride in the country."

She smiled back at him as she ducked under the hatch opening.

Jonathan Tairas was from Palus, the oldest and richest of Earth's colonial satellites, and there was about him, the envious said, the aura and the arrogance of the aristocrat. On long research missions, such as the Eridan Project, where isolation and loneliness sometimes created strange bonds, Tairas remained aloof, always at ease with his fellows but never intimate with anyone. Theo thought he had a good sense of self and of self-preservation. Both were qualities she admired and shared. She knew him only in a professional capacity, but what she knew of him she respected. He was that rare combination—a good scientist and a good administrator. But a good administrator did not act as an errand boy.

"May I ask why I am thus honored?"

He looked as if he were about to give a flippant answer, then

(61)

changed his mind. "You signaled for help. I wanted to be the first person to talk to you." He paused to get her reaction. She remained silent, waiting, noting new stress lines around his eyes, his disheveled uniform, hands that trembled slightly. "There is no easy way to say it so I will be blunt. I didn't know what mental state you would be in and I didn't want you to be terrified by wild stories. There has been a mutiny. The Expedition Commander is either dead or being held hostage. The Vice Commanders are missing. All discipline is gone at Base One."

"And with us? Base Three?"

"Our people are still disciplined, still sane. But morale is low. Between news of the mutiny and the fear and this greed—this 'gold fever'—for crystals . . ."

It all seemed to sadden him, Theo observed. He saw her studying him and he smiled self-consciously. "And you? Have you been well?" As if this were a social occasion, she thought. "It was the rain that prompted your call? I was wondering if we would hear from you. And I was planning to come look for you tomorrow if we did not. Of course I wouldn't have looked for you down here."

"It was the rain," she assured him. "Now, you said the Orlovs had disappeared. Do you know where—how?"

He shook his head. "There are rumors they were killed, other rumors that they fled with their daughter to the interior. I know the Orlovs; I cannot picture either of them acting with dishonor. . . ."

"They were brought out here," Theo said softly. She would not have guessed that he was so personally concerned about the Orlovs until she saw how his face lit with glad misunderstanding

(62)

and such relief that she felt sad to have misled him. "I am afraid what I must tell you . . ." she began, and related the pertinent events of that morning that now seemed so long ago. He listened, staring out at the rain. Tears he made no attempt to hide or check ran down his cheeks and glistened on his stubbly beard.

When she had said all that needed saying, she stopped. They sat silently together. The rain plinked on the roof above them. Theo looked over at the tent and wondered if Karen was awake and frightened. Tairas fumbled in his pockets for a tissue and, finding one, blew his nose. Tears continued to leak out, and he wiped them away with his fingertips.

"They were from Palus," he said after a time. "We were children together. And cousins. But then, it is such a small colony that all Paluvians are cousins. Elizabeth, Simon, and I . . . we were friends."

"And there are so many strangers," said Theo, and his eyes met hers. In their lives, unless those they loved traveled with them to other worlds, they were left behind in time and space. When one traveled the distance of light years, most good-byes were, by the laws of physics, final. It was a fact Theo had forced herself to live with. It brought with it the freedom of an anchorite, and the discipline.

"Come," she said, and stood up. "The rain is depressing us. And sitting here solves nothing."

As they came down the ramp, the tent flap bulged out and Karen emerged. At the sight of Jonathan Tairas she started to smile, then caught herself and looked to Theo for confirmation. "It's all right," the woman called. "He's safe." And Tairas looked at her in surprise.

(63)

"You distrusted me?" he said innocently, and then, reflectively, "Yes, I guess you would after what you've both seen."

His eyes narrowed and he studied Theo's face. "If the rains hadn't started, you'd have stayed out here?"

"I begged her to," said Karen. "Don't blame her. She wanted to call for help right away. But I was scared. Is it safe for me to go back?"

"As safe as it is for any of us." He stretched out his arms to Karen. "I am so glad to find you," he said and they exchanged a wet hug.

X

FROM the air Base Three looked like a sprinkle of puffball mushrooms that had sprung up in the shade of massive trees. The trees surrounded a small artesian-fed lake whose eastern bank spilled in a series of steep falls to the beach. Framed by mountains and edging the sea, the site was a pleasant one. In the enthusiasm of the first few weeks it had been nicknamed Paradise.

"How small it looks," Theo said when she saw it come into view. It seemed to her the camp had shrunk in the weeks of her absence, become more vulnerable to the endless miles of emptiness that surrounded it. "And deserted. Where is everybody? All the equipment?"

"Under domes to keep dry." He touched an intercom button

on his chair arm. "Control, this is Tairas. Open the hangar. We're coming in." There was no response and he repeated, "Control? Open the hangar!"

"Maybe they're still in bed?" suggested Karen. She strained against her belt to sit high enough to look down at the base, but the belt held her snugly, frustratingly.

"I don't see anyone outside," said Theo.

Preoccupied, Tairas did not answer. Updrafts from the ocean were giving the craft a final buffeting as it cruised slowly down to land. They were close enough to the ground for Theo to see the trees shaking in the wind. It occurred to her that she had never before seen their branches move on this normally quiet world.

"We'll land outside," Tairas announced. "We're going to get wet again."

"That's O.K. We're used to it," Karen said, and then, hesitantly, "Do you think anyone is going to . . . uh . . . do anything when they see me? Or afterward?"

"They will treat you with the respect due your rank," he said curtly, and the craft jerked upward as the airpods dropped. Theo glanced over at him and wondered if his barely concealed irritation was due to his inexpertise with the craft or the failure of his controller to reply. His entire manner had become formal once again. With seemingly one motion, he released his seat belt, opened the main hatch, and stood up. "Karen, Dr. Leslie—I have matters to attend to. We'll talk over lunch."

As the hatch dropped, the compartment filled with the scent of rain and wet soil. Theo inhaled greedily, glad to be on solid ground again. It was raining hard here; water poured down the

(66)

skin of the hangar dome; the wheel tracks that surrounded them were small rivers.

Jonathan Tairas strode down the ramp and disappeared behind the curve of the dome.

There was no sound other than the rain. She had not expected a reception committee, but it seemed to her that curiosity alone should have brought a few associates out to greet her. Evelyn Wexler and Philip, perhaps. But it had not. Suppressing a sigh, she collected Karen and her gear.

The two of them sloshed off toward the living quarters. As they came around the big central equipment dome, the wide tree-lined central avenue of the camp stretched down to the sea. Waves, deepened by clouds to almost coffee color, were rolling up on the shingle beach, and piles of foam were blowing in the wind.

"It's prettier up here than Base One is . . . was," Karen observed.

"Fewer people," said Theo distractedly.

There was something odd about this place. Or perhaps it was her imagination. It just didn't feel right. They saw no one during the long walk to the living quarters. The door of that dome hung half open in the wind, and the rain was beating in. She frowned · to herself. "Careless," she judged as she pushed her way into the lobby and turned to assure herself Karen was still with her. They stood dripping in the stillness, the carpet turning darker beneath them. Karen reached back and shoved the door shut. Rain lodged in the ball sockets of the hinges made a singing sound.

"Hello?" Theo called into the quiet.

"Maybe they're all on duty," suggested Karen.

"Why are you whispering?" whispered Theo, and then, in a

normal voice, "Let's open the tent in the gym to dry. Then we'll find you a compartment and some decent clothes. Come." She turned briskly and walked down the curving hall, feigning an ease she did not feel.

The building seemed so empty; she was beginning to suspect it was deserted. All mood lights were off leaving the walls white and bare. There was no music, no normal smells. In the stillness somewhere a ventilation fan whispered. For the first time she could hear the intermittent hush-hush-hush of the waves on the beach outside. Along the corridors privacy curtains were open, revealing unoccupied compartments. She hurried past them as if they were normal.

The wall speakers made the chiming sound that always preceded an announcement. "Dr. Leslie. Dr. Leslie." It was Tairas. Theo ran a few steps to the screen outside the gym. "Yes?"

"Are you two all right?"

"Yes, why?"

"Is the building empty?"

"It appears so. I haven't looked . . ."

"The entire camp's deserted. I can't find a soul. The land cruisers are missing."

"Aircraft?"

"Here. If they left by air, someone came and got them."

"Have you checked the log?"

"The last entry was mine at six this morning."

The staff was too professional, too well disciplined, to leave without making a log entry. She was silent for a moment, thinking, until she found enough courage to ask, "Are there any signs of violence?"

(68)

Now it was his turn for silence, and she guessed with a tinge of surprise that the thought had not occurred to him. "No. At least I haven't found any."

"So they left by choice."

"I don't think so." Karen's voice was small. "Look in the dining room."

One glance at Karen's face and Theo knew something wretched had happened. "I think you should come over here, fast," she told his image and clicked off. "What is it?"

Karen just shook her head.

Normally the most attractive place in the building, the dining room had one window wall overlooking the rocks and sea below. The carpeting was thick and green, the dining alcoves plush and private. Special lighting effects made textured patterns on walls and dome, and a Telarian-style fountain shimmered in the center of the room.

The fountain still shimmered. It was all that remained intact in the big space. A scummy foam danced on the fountain basin beneath the spray. The window had been crushed in. It lay in crystal-like bits over half the once-green carpet that was now black and sodden. The tables lay scattered, the velvet foam seats crushed to misshapen lumps. Scattered about among the debris were bulgy masses of wet pink rags. There was a sick-sweet smell in the room.

It seemed to Theo she had seen rags like that before. She stood in the doorway, staring, unable to absorb the idea, and there crept into her mind the image of the scavenger she had seen that morning. She saw it again over the fallen weejee—and what it left behind—and she knew she was going to be very sick. "What a mess," she said mildly, for Karen's benefit. "Uh . . . let's go to my compartment?"

"But what happened? Was there an explosion?"

Theo didn't have time. With a shrugging motion she dropped the pack to the floor with a clunk, grabbed Karen's hand, and literally pulled her down the hall after her to her room. With her free hand she pressed the node that opened the privacy curtain, saw the area was intact, and when they both crossed the threshold, she closed the curtain behind them.

"Sit there," she said briskly, pointing to her bed. "I'll be right back." And in the sanit module she hoped the rush of water screened the sound of her retching. But her concern at sparing Karen's sensibilities was mitigated by her own shock. "They were eaten," a small nagging tape kept replaying in her consciousness, "eaten and the husks spit out," and she would gag again.

"Here." A small hand grasped her chin, gently pulled her head back, and thrust something under her nose. There was a pop as the trauma-pac was squeezed. "Inhale slowly." There was a second popping sound. "Once more. Inhale." Theo found herself obeying. The minty gas felt good in her throat. She closed her eyes and laid her cheek against the cool rim. In a second a cold wet cloth was being pressed firmly against her forehead, another was fitted against the back of her neck and held there. "O.K. Sit up. Keep your eyes open. It helps the vertigo if you focus."

"Where did you learn all this?"

"I get very space sick. Inhale." The child was all business. In spite of her misery, Theo almost smiled; who was protecting whom from shock? "And quit trying to spare me," Karen told her. "I *know* what that is on the floor in there. Staff."

(70)

It took a little time for that last remark of Karen's to penetrate Theo's understanding. But when it did, she almost forgot her sickness. She should have known from the sight of Karen's face as she came back along the hall after first seeing the dining room. It was the same look Karen had had when she stepped into the flashlight's beam—the look of someone who is maintaining self-control by refusing to think or feel.

Theo recognized that look. She had seen it reflected in her mirror every morning for the first years after she left Earth. She knew what would have happened to her then if anyone had tried to penetrate the wall she had built around feeling.

Closing her eyes, she took a deep breath and considered this child who stood so still beside her. She couldn't be more than twelve. Where had she learned how to survive—or was it inherent, a matter of breeding?

"Why are you so quiet?" There was concern in Karen's voice. "Are you going to be sick again?"

"No . . . I'm better." Theo risked moving her head with her eyes open and looked up at her. "I was resting."

"O.K." Karen could accept that.

"Are you . . . as well as you can be?"

The girl's eyes narrowed slightly, and the grip tightened on the washcloth. "Yes . . . I feel . . ." Whatever she was going to say, she thought better of it, and deliberately directed her attention back to Theo. "Why don't you go in and lie down?"

Theo knew better than to press the issue. "All right," she said. "For a few minutes."

XI

AFTERWARD Theo could scarcely remember the details of that day. Her mind blurred them beyond feeling. They had attempted to contact both Base One and the Agribase. There was no response and no time to discover whether it was transmittal failure or climatic conditions or something else. They next armed themselves and searched all domes, for survivors and the creature or creatures who might have done this. They found neither. Electronic beam alarms were rigged around the lab and living domes.

There was no time for fear or grief or revulsion, any of the programmed emotional responses to death. The dining-room wreckage was filmed in detail, the necessary lab samples were taken, and then the room was cleared with a scoop dump. All debris was lasered to powdery ash on which the pelting raindrops seemed to explode before washing away in filmy rivulets.

She remembered it rained all day.

By midafternoon the computer had analyzed the tissue samples and identified the dead.

NAME	AGE	OCCUPATION	BIRTHPLACE
Kiharu Ito	24	Logistician	Sat. Belvieu, L₅
Genis Illian	31	Geologist	U.S.S.R., Earth
Adrian Haras	23	Meteorologist	Eufor, Mars
Hotra Van	29	Photographer	New York, Earth
Joan Lee	25	Geologist	Eufor, Mars
Luz Djamu	25	Oceanographer	U.S.S.R., Earth
Pun Li Chan	28	Ichthyologist	Sinkiang, Earth
Larry Samuels	32	Physicist	Ringworld, Saturn
Lindsay Shore	21	Nutritionist	Sat. Belvieu, L₅
Shar Olin	22	Master Mechanic	Sat. Titan, L₃
Robert Landau	26	Astrophysicist	Houtex, Earth
Seto Kim	29	Environmentalist	Ringworld, Saturn
Geoff Piedrahita	33	Computer Specialist	Bombay, Earth
William Roy	27	Master Mechanic	Sansuk, Mars

As the pictures followed one after the other across the vuscreen, the computer ended each biography with the words, "Deceased. KILOD, Eridan, ET March 15, 2763, Cause of Death unknown." It seemed to Theo the list would never end and that Commander Tairas would never stop murmuring, "Ah no, ah no."

The computer then attempted to analyze the foreign matter included with the tissue samples: amino acids, enzymes, mucoid tissues, hair particles, nonchitinous cuticle, soil, algae, bacteria, leaf fragments. The leaves were local, the algae and bacteria unknown. The soil had trace elements from an unidentified area of the planet. The balance of the items were from a creature or creatures unknown.

Somewhat to Commander Tairas's annoyance, Theo refused to speculate as to what sort of animal she thought it might be. "We have seen no predators," she said, "nothing resembling them. The only carnivores are scavengers. There have been more of those since the rains. For all I know this could be a glider, or a sea creature, or something I mistakenly called a browser. I haven't the foggiest what it is."

She could feel the tension in her jaws and hear the edge in her voice. Karen, asleep on the lounge under the window, stirred under the blankets of lab coats. "I'm sorry," Theo apologized. "My nerves are on edge. We all need some food and rest."

"Mine too. I apologize," he said. "I've been hungry for hours, but I frankly can't bear the idea of going into the dining room."

She nodded, understanding, and then remembered. "There's the serving outlet in the rec-room lounge."

It was decided there was little more they could accomplish in the lab in their present state of exhaustion, and, after making sure the intercom to the living dome was on night hookup, they went out for a walk to look around. The outside lights came on just as they stepped into the rain, and they saw water was coming down in sheets. The lake was spilling over with muddy water. Wind buffeted them and whipped the trees. Waves were rolling up the beach and uncurling in a giant pouring of energy. It was all the three of them could do to walk the distance to the next dome. They clung to one another for support.

"If those waves get much bigger, rain is going to be the least of our problems," Tairas yelled over the storm.

"The trees have been here a thousand years," Theo yelled back. "They weren't washed away."

"Keep away from the beam," Karen yelled at both of them, "or else we'll set off the alarm ourselves."

XII

TIRED as she was, Theo couldn't fall asleep that night. She wasn't aware of fear; she simply could not get her mind or her stomach to stop churning. The blanket was too tight over her feet. She loosened it. Her elbow itched. She scratched it. Then her nose itched. She rolled over and stuck a foot out for air. "Go to sleep," she told herself. "Stop thinking about it. Think about animals, all the new animals that come out in the rain. Ugly little things." She kept seeing the dead weejees in the grass and the odd creature feeding . . . there was a connection there . . . if only her mind would concentrate. She turned restlessly, shoved the pillow off the bed, and fell instantly asleep.

The mental anesthetic imposed by self-discipline was nullified by sleep. Her mind sorted and replayed in random sequence. One weird dream followed another, most of them unpleasant. When, halfway through the night, something touched her bed, she rolled violently away and reached for her laser.

"It's O.K. It's O.K.," came a hurried whisper. "It's me. Karen. You were yelling in your sleep. You woke me up."

"Sorry, didn't mean to scare you," Theo mumbled. "What was I saying?" It seemed very important somehow.

"Something about going to quit or going . . . it sounded like Kript."

"Crypt?" She remembered thinking the word . . . and tried to remember the dream, but it was gone. Except the image of the cavern. She shook her head. "I'm sorry I woke you. Go back to sleep."

Karen padded off obediently to her bed in the alcove. As soon as Theo saw her pull the blanket up, she let her eyes fall shut. "Crypt?" she thought. "Crypt? I must be more depressed than I thought."

It was daylight—or as light as it was going to get with the rain —when she woke again. She thought she heard voices outside and sat up to look out the window. All that was out there were trees, ocean, and rain. With a sigh she got up and went to the bathroom and came back to her bed. Karen was still sleeping. The clock said eight-thirty.

The alarm went off then—a high-pitched warble. A door slammed and muffled laughter came from the lobby. Karen's eyes popped open. The floor trembled with a series of thumps. There was a shout and a babble of softer voices. Theo grabbed the laser and slid out of bed.

(77)

"Maybe your staff is back?" suggested Karen.

"Maybe," was the whispered reply, "or maybe we have visitors from Base One."

Someone ran past her door and stopped suddenly. She tensed for trouble. The alarm stopped warbling. "Hi, Commander," called a man's familiar voice. "Why the gun?"

"We thought you might be angry, but not like this," called another. There was more laughter, but not a sound from Jonathan Tairas.

"Wait until we show you what we found!" That voice Theo definitely recognized; it was Evelyn Wexler, who headed their medical staff. She opened her door and stepped into the hall, to be greeted with a glad cry of "Theo! You're back! We were worried about you. Out there by yourself in all that rain. We were just saying, coming back, that if you hadn't called—we were going to go look for you. Let me hug you!" The tall Earth woman pulled her close in a wet embrace, and over Evelyn's shoulder Theo saw Commander Tairas.

He was in the grip of that anger that overtakes us when we have waited and worried too long about someone, only to discover they were in no danger at all and simply forgot to let us know where they were. His famous self-control was in danger of disappearing.

"May I ask where you people have been?" His voice was too quiet, and he was paying far too much attention to the simple task of putting his gun back in its holster.

"Crystal hunting," said Dr. Felix. "We all went crystal hunting. Except maybe twenty comfort lovers who couldn't be lured into the rain by the promise of wealth." He frowned. "They told you where we were?"

"No," Tairas said softly. "They did not. Why didn't you make a log entry?"

"It wasn't necessary. Everybody here knew we had . . ."

"Did you all . . . come back together?" asked Theo.

"Yes," Evelyn answered. "Some of the greedier ones wanted to stay out another day since the hunting was so good, but this awful weather . . ." She looked from the Commander's face to Theo's. "What is it? Why was the alarm set? What happened here?"

"Trouble from Base One?" someone guessed.

"Why didn't they tell you where we went?" persisted Evelyn.

Tairas and Theo exchanged glances. "I didn't ask them," he said. "Mr. Maxwell, will you please see to it that the alarm is reset immediately. Now! If you will excuse me, I have an announcement to make." And he left them.

"Has there been trouble?" Evelyn asked and frowned at Theo's laser.

"Yes. Quite serious trouble," Theo admitted. "But I think I should let the Commander explain what happened."

Before anyone could say anything, the speakers chimed throughout the complex of domes.

"This is Commander Tairas. There will be a general staff meeting in Conference Room A at nine a.m. You will be there. You will be dressed for work detail. You will be armed. Our main dining room is temporarily closed. Please breakfast in the lounge. The maintenance staff will report to my office immediately."

As he spoke more people came into the dome. They could be

(79)

heard murmuring in the lobby, dropping packs on the floor, shaking rain capes, some coming down A Hall to their rooms, others going down B Hall.

To avoid further questions, Theo glanced at her watch. "It's eight-forty now. We don't have much time," she said, and escaped into her room. "How is he going to tell them what happened here?" she wondered. Just how did one approach conveying that sort of news to one's colleagues?

Conference Room A occupied the center of the circular dome. It was a large round room, spartanly equipped with tables, velvet foam cubes for seating, vu-screen, and data terminals.

The staff was still hurrying in when the Commander entered. Theo noted, with approval, that he had shaved and changed.

"Would you all be seated, please? Let me begin by saying how truly glad I am to see you again. What you are about to learn will be traumatic to all of you, some more so than others. For that reason I suggest you each take one of these trauma-pacs and keep it handy in case you need it."

"Are you going to tell us the bottom fell out of the gem market, Jon?" called one of the engineers, and there was nervous laughter. Tairas ignored the remark. A tense quiet fell in the high-domed room as the box of drug packets passed from hand to hand.

"I shall begin at the beginning. I was on duty as controller, Monday morning at six, when Dr. Leslie signaled for pickup. I went out to meet her. As peripheral information, you should know that Dr. Leslie and I also brought back Karen Orlov, the daughter of the Expedition co-directors. Her parents have been killed by the rebel factions. Orlov minor will remain here as our guest." This was greeted with sympathetic murmurings mixed with indignation and a few crisp "damn savages." "We returned at noon. The base was deserted—"

"Impossible. There were at least twenty . . ." Evelyn's voice died away as Tairas's dark eyes fixed on her.

"To get on with my story," Tairas continued, "when the three of us returned, the base appeared totally deserted." He paused and then plunged into telling the events of the day before as quickly and as gently as he could. After a warning of its shock possibility, one frame of an over-all view of the dining room was shown.

There was a shocked silence, then the room filled with voices. It took the Commander some little time to restore order. Several people hurried from the room.

"Commander Tairas?" Evelyn waved to be recognized. "I think I should report that this is not the first time several of us have seen . . . evidence like this. Felix and I found something like that in a crevasse in the foothills yesterday. Water was rushing over it, so it was difficult to see clearly. And frankly we didn't study it long. . . ."

"Do you know what sort of animal did it?" asked Theo.

"I do." The voice came from the other side of the table. All heads turned to Philip. "Or at least I think I do. It's enormous. . . ."

"Let's have the complete story, please," said Tairas.

"I was up on a small ledge. I'd found a lot of crystals washed out of a cave. You could pick them up by the handful." Tairas frowned and Philip dropped the subject of crystals. "Anyhow, there came this herd of yellow grass-eaters down below, running. I'd never seen any of these animals run, so I watched to see what scared them. And then I saw two big hairless things come around the hill. They must have been fifteen feet long, half that high, brown, a lot of stubby legs with long, cruel claws and a funny blunt head and bug eyes. Big as they were, they could really move! And they are smart. You could tell by the way they herded the animals into a cul-de-sac. One blocked the exit and the other went in, slashing hell out of the victims with those claws. They rear up, like caterpillars. . . . Excuse me . . . but it was cruel to see. They killed the whole herd. Then that orange mouth opened and sort of sucked in a dead animal. I wanted to run, but I was afraid they would see me. There was only one way off the ledge, and if they saw me . . . I wasn't armed. I waited until they finished feeding and left—before I moved."

"Did the victims look like that?" The dining-room still shot appeared on screen.

"Yes, Commander." Philip put his hands over his face.

"You said nothing to your companions?"

"I didn't want to leave all those crystals, all that money just lying there . . . for somebody else."

Tairas sighed. But then he had been born to great wealth. "And you, Dr. Wexler, and Dr. Felix, you also kept silent?"

They both nodded.

Theo heard little of this. Her mind was still going over what Philip had said. On a hunch she stood up. "Commander Tairas, may I be excused to get some tapes from my pack? You wanted me to speculate on what this creature might be. I'm ready to do that now. Philip, don't go away. I want you to see these. Oh, one more thing, may I bring Karen Orlov back with me?"

The Commander nodded. "While Dr. Leslie is gone, let's discuss what we can do to increase our security here."

(82)

XIII

OFF in a cloud of excited speculation about the mystery
animal, the sight of staff members crying in the hall surprised
Theo and made her feel guilty. She had forgotten. "Am I really
so totally unfeeling?" she wondered. "We found them and I
didn't cry. Neither did the Commander or Karen. Are we all
three space children, so long and so far removed from Earth that
we are no longer quite human?"

Then a voice sobbed, "I don't want to die out here," and Theo's
lip curled in wry amusement. Was it grief for the dead—or fear
for their own lives that caused the weeping? It really didn't matter; neither emotion helped solve this or any other problem. She
turned and ran down the hall to her compartment.

"Karen!" she called as she burst in. "Where did we put the pack?"

"I unpacked it. What's wrong?" Karen put down her book. "What's happening at the meeting?"

"The film we took in the cave that day—where's the recorder?"

"I'll get it."

"One of the men saw an animal that sounds like the ones you found."

"The mummies?" Karen pulled the oblong unit down from a shelf and handed it to Theo. "Where?"

"Chasing grazers in the foothills."

"You mean alive?" The girl stared at her. "Alive?" *That* animal?"

"It sounds like it." She took the recorder from its case.

"How can that be?"

Theo shrugged. "I don't know yet. Come. Let's go show these to him."

"Am I allowed to come now? I thought I was too young for the meeting."

Theo grinned down at her, thinking of the weepers in the hall, and said, "You're a lot older than most of the staff. Besides, I want your claim to fame established now, at the beginning, so there is no question of this creature's discoverer."

"You think it's going to be *that* important?"

"Probably not. But I think you will be," was Theo's cryptic reply as they entered the conference room.

She waited until the Commander had finished what he was

saying and turned to her. "Dr. Leslie. You had something you wanted to show us?"

"Yes, something Karen Orlov found. Ladies and gentlemen, Karen Orlov." Karen bowed to the assembly and slipped shyly into the chair next to Theo's.

The biologist extracted the coin-sized tape and fitted it carefully into the projector part of the table. She touched several buttons on the terminal, one to enlarge, one to record into the permanent data banks, and another to record simultaneously on research data banks and their daily log files. The computer's voice confirmed its readiness to ingest all this information. On its screen appeared a picture of the view from Theo's camp.

"Look. It's not raining," someone said, and there was laughter in the room.

"It does seem remarkable, doesn't it?" said Theo. "This film was shot at my camp in the mountains. The area is vegetation poor, as you can see. The air is very dry, desert-like. Altitude approximately seven thousand feet." The camera wide-panned and picked up two vots starring in toothy curiosity.

"That's not the vicious animal I saw," said Philip, and there was more laughter. Theo shut off the film. Somewhere soon on that tape were the pictures of Karen's parents. "I've shown you this to introduce the general area." She removed that tape and inserted the next. "Now I'll show you where the animal was found." The screen showed the approach to the cave. "This is about ten miles southwest of my camp."

"Look at the crystals!"

"You'll never be poor, Leslie. How many did you bring back?"

"Note what appears to be an established path." Theo ignored them. "Now, Philip, look closely at this." She stopped the tape and enlarged the frame.

"Look at those claws!"

"That thing's dead."

"Dried up."

"Does it resemble what you saw, Philip?" Theo persisted.

"It's hard to say in that lighting. The color is wrong. Too light. But it was something like that. The claws are just what I saw. How big was that?"

"It was curled up in a ball," said Karen, forgetting her shyness in the excitement of seeing her discovery again, "so you couldn't really tell its length. Not dried up like that. And we couldn't see its head to tell what kind of eyes it had. The animal was almost totally buried in the sand when we first saw it, except where the wind had blown sand away. But it was color banded. Like a caterpillar."

"Yes! Yes!" The young man grinned at her. "That's what it looked like! It even moved that way. You were aware of all the legs."

"*What* is a caterpillar, Dr. Leslie?" Evelyn asked for the benefit of people born in the satellites who had no practical knowledge of insects.

Theo explained briefly.

"You aren't going to tell me that's a larval form?" Evelyn said, aghast.

"Oh, no. It's a mature animal. Or at least I think it is . . ."

"Excuse me, Dr. Leslie," Commander Tairas interrupted. "This

(86)

is all very interesting, but how does it relate to the living animal Philip saw? If at all?"

"Look at this." Theo turned the film on again. "See those mounds? Each is a creature like the one Karen uncovered—"

"Look at the crystals!" and attention was again momentarily diverted.

"What is my point?" Theo wondered, because she didn't really know. Intuition told her it was the same type of animal. But how?

"Forget the damn crystals!" Tairas ordered. "Doctor?"

"The creatures all lay there in their crypt. . . ." Her dream of the night before came back suddenly at the word "crypt," and she sat there, staring at the Commander's eyes but seeing instead the cave and myriad other psychic symbols. "Cryptobiosis." She almost whispered the word. "Cryptobiosis. That's what my dream was telling me . . . but is it possible in so large a form?"

"Dr. Leslie? What are you talking about?" Commander Tairas spoke gently as if he suspected she had been suddenly overcome by nervous exhaustion.

"They may be the same animal," she said, "in a cryptobiotic state. I will explain. Cryptobiosis means hidden life. It is a state of suspended animation. The organism's activity slows down and eventually stops when its environment becomes too dry. It resumes animation when adequate moisture returns. This return to life is called anabiosis."

"Wasn't something like this tested in early deep space travel?" asked Tairas. "As I recall, Earth tried to freeze-dry astronauts— as we were called in those days."

(87)

"Correct," said Theo. "If it could have been done, the advantages would have been tremendous. In a cryptobiotic state, organisms can withstand any gravitational force, extreme temperature change, high vacuum, ionizing radiations . . . but in laboratory-induced cryptobiosis, desiccated tissue, especially neural tissue, did not respond properly to revival techniques. I remember reading an old study of the experiments. It was barbaric. Horrible!

"The rapid loss of water from an organism causes death," Theo went on. "But if dried slowly enough, theoretically body weight in water can be lost until water content of the tissue is less than three per cent. All activity stops. The body contracts. Without a specific carbohydrate molecule in unique proportion, death results. But with that carbohydrate molecule, suspended animation occurs. And with the addition of moisture, the body revives. The creature *returns to life.*"

"How long can an organism survive in this state?" asked Evelyn.

"It depends. Under ideal conditions, one year or one hundred Earth years would mean nothing to a cryptobiotic organism. It could be revived and redesiccated repeatedly. This planet may represent ideal conditions."

"Are you saying they're immortal?"

"No. I'm saying that, theoretically, cryptobiosis enables an organism to prolong its normal life-span almost indefinitely with periods of suspended activity. But the organism can be destroyed in either state, should you so desire."

"Do you seriously consider your theory feasible?" asked Tairas.

(88)

"Do you think those"—he indicated the pictures—"are capable of coming back to life?"

"I have seen stranger things," she said. "There's a very easy way to check it out. Let me take an air car and go up there and look at the cave. If it's still full of this—I'm wrong."

"I want to go along," Karen and Philip said in unison.

The Commander said, "That's a bad flight in good weather. And what if you are correct?"

"To find a creature of this size that's cryptobiotic. . . ?" She stared through him, thinking of what it might mean. If those molecules could be isolated—synthesized—with metabolic advances, lifetimes could be extended beyond human dreams perhaps. But who would want that? Aware he was waiting for a practical reply, she said, "For one thing, we'd know what we were fighting. There are enough problems with this expedition without the added jeopardy of becoming a protein source for a voracious beast."

XIV

"IF you're right, going back to the cave would be dangerous," Evelyn warned. "Those creatures might kill you."

"If I'm right, the cave will be empty," said Theo. "If it is empty, the next question is: how many other caves like that exist, and how many creatures?"

There was a sudden silence in the room.

"Very well." Tairas sat up straighter. "We will cordon the base with alarms and laser fire. Guards will be posted. Does anyone object to serving guard duty?"

No one did. "Dr. Leslie, I want to know more about these animals—or know more definitely our degree of danger. You will be allowed a staff of three to solve the problem. Please let me know by lunchtime how you propose to handle the matter. Now, we are suffering from communications problems. I want you technicians to check out our transmitter. I would like to talk to the Agribase as soon as possible. Dr. Wexler?"

"Has there been any contact with Base One? Do you know if they've contacted any ship of our fleet or received any reply to their demands?"

"No. To both questions." He studied the worried faces around the table. "If you are concerned about being stranded on Eridan forever . . . don't be. The Aurora Corporation does not waste people in whom it has so much invested. Regardless of what happens at Base One, we will be picked up. At present, we have two major objectives: First to stay alive and healthy. Second, to function as the professionals we are. This is, as you know, a business venture. We have a duty to protect and salvage as much as possible the money invested in this feasibility study. This world may be colonized. It depends on our work."

"Are we going back to the caves?" Karen wanted to know as soon as the meeting ended and the staff was filing out.

Theo nodded, her mind on something else. Tairas was right. Eventually the space shuttle would return for them. All that happened here would be under inquiry. Considering the unorthodoxy of the situation, it was probable that all expedition members would be confined to one base or even one cruiser until judgment was made. It would be prudent of her to feed all her tapes into the data banks now. But she didn't want Karen to see and relive again part of that film. She sat looking at Karen's face, staring through her, wondering what excuse she should devise to get her out of the room while the tapes and journal were being recorded.

"What is it?" the girl asked. "You don't want me to go along?"

"Oh, no—I promised you. . . . No. What I was thinking . . ." Her focus narrowed to see the girl again; Karen . . . who did not take kindly to lies. . . . "What I was thinking was that I must record my tapes and notes into the computer. Some of it will be painful for you. I would prefer that you don't see it."

"You filmed my parents?"

"Yes."

"The killing? The whole thing?"

"Yes, if the night lens picked it up."

Karen looked down at the blue carpet and nodded. "Good," she said. "And no, I don't want to see that. Not ever again." She slid to her feet. "I'll go see what the Commander wants me to do." At the door Karen stopped and stood thinking.

"Theo? Let's call them cave bears."

"Call whom?"

"The mummies we found. They need a name—we can't just keep calling them 'those things' or stuff like that. We found them in a cave and they're bigger than bears, so let's call them cave bears."

"Very well. They're cave bears."

XV

THEO had more volunteers than she had expected for the trip back into the mountains. Their enthusiasm puzzled her. When she first went alone into the interior, half the base staff had been so incapacitated by illogical fear that they had had to escort each other from dome to dome. They were afraid to be alone outside. Now, with several very good reasons to be afraid, almost no one was. Why? They could ignore the danger of the rain, flying in the rain, the threat of the animal, the discomfort of camping out? She too was worried about all these things, but her sense of curiosity was stronger than her sense of fear. "I don't understand my popularity," she told Karen after the fourteenth volunteer left their compartment.

Karen looked at her oddly and frowned. "You really don't know why they want to go with you?"

Theo shook her head.

"Remember when the pictures of the cave started? No one said, 'Look at the mounds!' What they said was, 'Look at the crystals!' "

"Oh, surely not greed. Not to *that* degree," Theo said in her naïveté.

"The Commander said rumor has it that the crystals are worth twelve hundred credits per karat uncut. Some of the crystals weigh more than twenty-five hundred karats."

"Oh." Theo did not question what they would do with the money. She realized her attitude toward money was not mainstream. Like all members of colonial research and development crews, she was unable to spend any of her salary in space or while confined to new planets. Credits accumulated and interest compounded until, short of insane extravagance, she would never have time to spend it all. When she finally retired, probably to one of the ringworlds where controlled environments and lessened gravity prolonged human life, she would live to a ripe, rich old age. As should all her colleagues. The fact that almost all of them seemed to feel that one could never have too much money puzzled her. At times it made her wonder if they knew something she did not.

"Well," she said, "they can risk their lives to pick up crystals. But not mine or yours. We're going alone, you and I."

Karen fell asleep early. The base was very quiet that evening. It seemed odd to look out the windows and see all the lights outside—odd but comforting. They lit up the rain. No animals at all even approached the area. Those staff members not on guard duty kept to their own rooms. Theo, busy collecting what gear she would need for the trip, saw almost no one in the halls after eight p.m.

In the deserted lounge the vu-screen was entertaining the chairs with a very hoary space opera. She turned it off. From the sounds escaping into the hall, it was evident that a therapy session was going on in Dr. Wexler's quarters. Evelyn was a devout believer in body contact to relieve tension and depression. Theo did not wonder why she had not been invited. She knew. But she did wonder for a moment if the Commander was in therapy, since Dr. Wexler had been trying to convince him it would be beneficial. And then Theo forgot about therapy as the thought occurred that it might be handy to have a large saw to cut up a sample specimen—provided there were still specimens to be cut up.

She was lugging the saw out to the lobby to add it to the equipment to be loaded in the morning when Commander Tairas came in. Water puddled off his cape. For some reason she was very glad to see he had been outside.

"I made sure the work wagon was all in order for you. Gave you the new one. Loaded your equipment. Old Tom Carlyle knew his stuff—know thy work and do it. The dictum certainly produces contented biologists, even at this hour." He swung off the cape and hung it neatly over a chair back. "Come. Stop working for tonight and have a cube of coffee with me. Or shall I help you bring out more equipment first?"

"I'm done," she assured him, setting the saw down. "Last piece."

He raised an eyebrow at the saw but didn't ask why she needed it.

"Who's going with you?"

"Karen."

"And?" His whisker stubbles rasped as he rubbed his wet cheek on his sleeve.

"Just Karen." She saw he was going to argue. "She's the only one I can count on not to spend time picking up crystals. I can't afford to have someone who will be distracted by greed. It's too dangerous."

"I'll go with you," he said impulsively.

She shook her head. "You would be court-martialed for leaving your command for such a reason as this. Know thy work and do it, remember? I'm the biologist. You are the Commander of this group. We are all your responsibility."

"Yes, but you get to have all the fun and I have to stay here and baby-sit." He was joking and yet he was not, because he added wistfully, "I really would like to see that cave, Theo. I suppose you are right, though—about taking more than two. They'd just be added weight in the air and worry on the ground. But how about Philip instead of Karen? It is a dangerous situation for a—"

"No!" She was very positive about that. "If I left without her, even for the best of reasons, she would never forgive me. She told me once it didn't matter how things got spoiled—once it was done you couldn't ever make it right again. I'm not going to spoil this for her." Or for myself either, she thought, remembering the touching trust of this child.

Tairas looked skeptical. "I'm not sure I understand all that.

Since it's you, I'll go along with it. But I want both of you to wear intercoms all the way out, during, and back. You'll be monitored. . . ."

Theo gave him her sweetest smile. She had no intention of wearing an electronic eavesdropper, but there was no point in telling him that. "Oh, yes!" She'd just thought of it. "My lab pack! The power cell in the microscope died on me. Is there another one around?" He thought a minute, nodded, and they set off to find it. The subject of monitoring was forgotten.

XVI

WHEN Theo came outside in the morning, the rain splattered against her hood. She found Karen and Tairas standing by the already loaded aircraft. In spite of the rain they were surrounded by half the people in camp. For a bad instant she thought something had happened.

"I just quit worrying quite so much about you, Dr. Leslie," the Commander called. "Why didn't you tell me your colleague had laser vision?" Theo's perplexity must have shown on her face because he laughed. "I was going to give Karen some parental instruction on self-defense," he explained, "until she made me look like an awkward amateur. Show her, Karen."

Karen looked up at Theo, her eyelashes jeweled with rain. "I used to practice targets a lot when we traveled. And on Coreco there were biting insects—like flying roaches. I used to shoot them." She sounded almost apologetic. "Want to see?"

"Very much," said Theo, and then saw that Karen held the most lethal gun the base was allowed.

"See that far branch jerking in the wind?" said Karen, pointing, and when Theo located the target down by the ocean, "Watch." Without bothering to sight, the girl raised the weapon and fired from waist level. There was a streak of blue. The branch dropped into the roiling water below. "See the one next to it?" The second branch dropped.

"Excellent," breathed Theo, who needed a rock to rest that weapon on before she could hit a target the size of a cup. "You're really excellent!"

Karen grinned. "Yes," she said, then calmly turned off the gun and handed it to the Commander. "Can we go now?"

"You're sure you won't change your mind, Dr. Leslie?" Philip was all dressed to go in case she had. She had not, and as she noted the geologist's bags stuffed in his belt, she was glad she had not.

"No. Thank you." She opened the hatch and stepped aside for Karen to get in out of the rain.

"Don't be greedy, Philip," Dr. Wexler said soothingly. "It's her find, hers and Karen's. We can find our own. There's plenty."

Theo's glance met Karen's, whose look said, "See?"

"They're not going for crystals." There was an edge of irritation in Tairas's voice. He handed the weapon to Theo. "I'd let Karen wear it, but it's too heavy for her. But when you go into the cave, you let her carry it. You'll both be safer."

"You've seen me shoot, huh?" Theo said, and he nodded.

(99)

"Now you should be pretty safe in this cabin." He pointed toward what appeared to be a belt of chain mail encircling the outer hull of the craft. Made of flexible optical fiber, each gleaming stud was a laser. "I had heavy-duty power cells put in. The mesh could hold a firing of thirty minutes. If it has to. It will heat up the interior but not beyond endurance. Your lethal range is maybe one hundred and fifty feet. . . ."

"Where is the switch?" Theo asked. "Just in case. I don't expect to need it." His eyebrow went up in disbelief. "No. Really. I think the cave and all the area around will be empty. There's no food up there."

"There are a lot of vots," said Karen from the front seat.

"But they're so small. It would be like a leopard hunting mice —" She saw the lack of understanding of this simile on the faces around her. "In any event, you're all getting wet. We'll see you in several days at the most. If the cave is empty, we'll be back by evening."

It seemed to her the good-byes and good advice took forever, but at last she could shut the hatch and turn the power on.

Within seconds after lift-off the camp below disappeared. Everything disappeared. There were no mountains, no sea, no heaven, and no planet. Only themselves in this fragile container rising up through the clouds, buffeted by wind gusts.

Theo sat tensely watching the altimeter and prayed that all systems were functioning perfectly. The craft was on autopilot. She had charted their course and programmed it into the craft's navigation system. Now she found herself wondering if she had marked the cave at the right place on the map. If not, could she make a manual landing in this weather? Just then they hit an air pocket and dropped with sickening swiftness before the craft recovered itself. She glanced over at Karen who got space sick.

"I'm fine," said Karen. "I took an antigrav tablet when I got up. The medic was a little mad when I woke her for it. It makes you anxious, doesn't it?"

"About the medic being mad?" said Theo, deliberately mis-understanding. "No. She probably had therapy last night," and she grinned.

Once the craft gained enough elevation to clear the coastal mountain chain, they moved inland. The turbulence from the ocean subsided. It was replaced by turbulence over the moun-tains. Neither felt talkative. The cabin was dark. Rain streaked across the windows. Their only idea of the terrain below came from tracings of the sonarscope.

"Why don't you take a nap?" Theo suggested once.

"I might miss something," said Karen. Theo repressed a smile.

Two and a half hours after lift-off they began to come down. The view outside was still solid cloud. The screen showed cliffs alarmingly close. They came in at slow speed. At three hundred yards the landing pods dropped. The clouds began to look more wispy. Then, peering out, she saw the ground dimly visible, dark red, rocks shining wet.

With a sigh of relief she put the controls on manual and flew a careful reconnaissance. Karen unsnapped her seat belt and stood up to peer out at the ground. In the five minutes or more in which they circled the cave, nothing moved on the ground but water. They landed below and to the right of the cave entrance.

XVII

SILENCE. A total absence of sound. It settled around them, cold, damp, immense. They stood in the open doorway, held there by this presence. For the moment the rain had stopped. There was almost no wind. Clouds layered overhead, trailing lethargic wisps.

"Listen," Karen whispered, and moved closer. Theo put an arm around her. Slowly, as their ears adapted to this new dimension, they heard the voices of water and soil, murmurings, trickles, irrhythmic drippings. Something in those sounds made the humans' skin crawl. "Come, let's get our gear together," said Theo.

Where there was no stone underfoot, it was slow walking. Rain turned the red soil to clay. Every step was a sloppy squelch. Pounds of mud clung to each boot and had to be stomped off on the next rock. Their joint approach to the cave was anything but silent.

From a safe distance away Karen stopped and stood ready with the gun. Theo climbed a rock and aimed a powerful torch into the black crevice. Nothing lurked in the front of the cave. She moved so that the light would penetrate the tunnel. They stood still for ten minutes or more, waiting, listening, hearts beating faster with the tension. The light flushed nothing out.

Theo waved to Karen to signal step two of their prearranged plan. Karen would remain where she was, as guard; Theo would approach close enough to throw a noise bomb into the cave.

With the clay sucking at her feet, Theo moved up. If the noise frightened any large creature out, it would be difficult to run in this. She hoped that in those circumstances Karen would not get buck fever and freeze. Trusting to instinct, she pressed the pin, threw, and began to back away. The bomb flashed a brilliant red, and its bang echoed in the hollow chamber. Again they waited.

"I was right," Theo called. "It's empty."

"Or they're still mummies," Karen reminded her.

"Or they're still mummies."

Even so Theo shifted the torch to her left hand and carried her gun in the right. The two of them entered the cave mouth from opposite sides. The sandy floor of the outer chamber was wet and hard-packed as a stream bottom. The footprints they made now were the only tracks there. Theo began to relax.

"Uh-oh." Karen pointed. The remains of the noise grenade lay

(103)

perhaps a third of the way up the sloping tunnel into the inner chamber. They had forgotten the slope. The two of them looked at each other.

"What do you think?" said Theo.

"Got another bomb?"

"Right."

Although the reverberating noise startled them, it produced no other results. They walked up the tunnel, feeling secure.

"It's still there!" Karen's torch played over a mound on the sandy floor. "Do you think the damp is rotting it?"

Theo took a slow, deep breath through her nose and wished she had not. "It's not . . . doing it any good," she said. She switched her light to wide beam to check the rest of the chamber. The stone walls had looked pale before; now they were bright red with dampness. The floor had been hilly with sandy mounds. Now it was pocked with hollows that shadowed in the light. She walked around the chamber to make sure.

"They *are* gone," she said, no triumph in her voice. "They are *gone.*" She could hardly believe it and stood lost in wonder that her suspicions had proved to be fact.

". . . gone too." She heard Karen without hearing her.

"Who?"

"The crystals. They're all gone too."

"Maybe sand washed over them," Theo suggested absently. "It looks like a river of water came through here." She was still puzzling over the idea of anabiosis for a bulk like this.

Using her boots as scrapers, Karen began searching at the edge of the nearest depression. "There were five or six heavy crystals here. I remember. They're not here now."

(104)

Theo frowned. "I don't think anyone else has been here—unless someone from our base flew up here last night. Which would be very dangerous . . . but not impossible." She shook her head. "The crystals are a minor detail we can worry about later," she decided. "Let's look at our friend here and see why it got left behind."

"Why didn't it go with the rest, do you think?"

"I *think* because we exposed it," Theo said. "We removed the sand. You will note the left side, which we could not lift out of the sand, has reconstituted? The right, the side exposed, has not. The water ran off too quickly for the dry tissue to absorb it evenly."

"So we really killed it?"

"In a broad sense," Theo agreed. "From the smell I would guess it died of gangrene. Does that make you sorry?"

Karen shook her head. "Not after seeing the dining room," she said.

An hour passed in preparation. Lighting and recording camera were rigged, equipment carried in from the work wagon, tarps spread over the sand, a folding table set up for the microscope and instruments, rubber suits and gloves put on.

It was a definite relief to put on the filter helmets. Along with the dust and microbes they eliminated odors in the air. The one remaining cave bear smelled a bit heady, so much so, in fact, that Theo had kept the direct lights off it, thinking even their faint heat would increase the scent.

As she checked Karen's helmet to make sure it was securely fastened at the throat, their eyes met through the plastic face masks and she saw something was wrong.

(105)

"What is it? Can't you breathe?"

"I can breathe O.K. . . . It's . . . I feel so alone in here."

Theo nodded her own bubble-enclosed head. "It's isolating," she agreed, "but necessary. Once we get to work you won't notice it as much." She gestured toward the specimen. "Shall we, Dr. Orlov?"

"O.K., Dr. Leslie."

Theo reached over and turned on the light.

The creature was almost twice as large as it had been before and no longer curled into a rounded shape. It lay stretched out, head exposed, skin smoothed and peppered with pores. The three legs on the top side, the side away from the sand, were still curled and withered, their claws grotesquely large. The legs below were fully extended, like a sponge enlarged by water. The abdomen was misshapenly swollen either by liquids or gas or both. Only the head seemed to have absorbed moisture at an even flow. It was cushion-round, large eyed, with a most peculiar mouth. Theo was about to squat down to have a closer look at the mouth and the lip apparatus in particular.

"Don't!" Karen grabbed her arm with a force that pulled Theo off balance and swung her back, away from the body, before letting go. Karen grabbed the gun from the table. As she pointed it at the dead thing, Theo yelled, "Don't burn it!"

"Its eye moved! It's not all dead!"

Theo looked at the saucer-sized eye. It was open and focused on Karen.

XVIII

LIKE a sick thing half wakened from fever dreams, the creature did not move. After regarding Karen blankly, its head shifted, with great effort. Its eyes scanned the cave and came to rest on Theo. Then, as if helpless to stop it, the head fell back onto the sand; leathery opaque eyelids slid down.

The whole thing took less than thirty seconds from the time Karen pounced until Theo regained her balance and stood erect. "Back away," she said softly to the girl. "I don't think it can stand up, but . . ." She put her hands on Karen's shoulders and guided her until they were in the tunnel mouth.

The animal made a noise then, a great sucking sort of snuffle. Karen turned her head away, and Theo found herself wanting to gag because she could visualize the condition of a respiratory system that produced a sound like that. Instead she watched carefully as spasms shook the creature's body. Its eyes opened again—and searched until it found them.

"Is it in pain?" Karen's whisper was almost inaudible through the helmet.

"I don't know."

"It's still dying?"

"Yes."

"Poor animal."

To her surprise Theo found her eyes filling with tears. Since the mask prevented brushing them away, she had to blink furiously. It was dangerous not to see clearly at this moment. "Why am I crying for this?" she wondered, and then admitted to herself the real cause of her tears. And stopped them.

"Think about it later," she said. Her normal voice was loud enough to echo in the chamber.

Startled, the animal snorted and jerked its head up. The short claw arm and left front leg flayed the sand and found leverage. With a groan it raised the shoulder of its bulk and faced them. Both eyes lit up with eagerness—to kill, or perhaps to communicate. Its mouth opened and the jaws moved, but no sound came out. The body jerked; the tongue bulged, and the creature vomited up two small yellow crystals. It stared at the crystals for a moment, as if surprised. Then suddenly, with desperate energy, it tried to push its ruined body toward them, the claw arm and three wizened legs audibly flopping. Once, twice, then abruptly, as if a life switch had been turned off, it collapsed and rolled sideways, dead.

The two people stood silent, watching the great eyes film. Finally Karen gave a little shrug and went and laid the gun on the table. "I'm going outside for a while," she announced and trudged off down the tunnel. Theo's helmet bubble bobbed assent.

"If you're going to be sick, take off the helmet."

In spite of her own revulsion, she found the cave bear fascinating. It was a carnivore, the first she had seen here. Radulae lined the great lips like a drill. The jaws were lined with very efficient shredders, the tongue and cheek cavity with acid sacs. It apparently fed by puncturing the victim, pouring on acid, and pumping out the solution. None of Eridan's animals was capable of much speed, and this thing could probably outrun them. Those short upper armlike things were grippers. The claws were cruelly efficient.

The creature was large and awkward to handle. Theo worked rapidly but with great thoroughness. Samples of each different tissue went into opaque specimen bags and into the cryogenic unit for instant freezing. The idea of staying here another day was not appealing. She would run all tests in the base lab.

The crystals were more of a mystery than ever. She picked up one with the tongs and studied it against the light. It dripped something, acid or saliva. Its surface was curiously etched. She dropped both crystals into separate noncorrosive vials and sealed them. Had the starving creature swallowed them in its death agony? Or were they like human gallstones?

"Wait until the people back there find out what kind of gems they've been collecting."

Theo jumped and nearly dropped the vials.

"I'm sorry. I didn't mean to scare you," Karen apologized. "It's

(109)

raining again." She looked at the remains of the creature and quickly looked away. "I came back to help. . . ."

Theo checked the face behind the helmet bubble and remembered her own reaction to her first autopsy. She had passed out cold and clammy. "Will you forgive me if I do it myself?" she said. "I know it's pure selfishness, but I concentrate better alone on a job like this."

Karen at first appeared willing to buy this line. Then a slow grin spread across her face. "I know you," she said. "You're afraid I'll throw up."

"Uh-huh," Theo said. "I did the first time. Would you prefer carrying those bags there out to the freezer in the work wagon? It's the green box on the left—"

"And it's marked 'frozen.' "

"Right."

"I'll find it. Trust me." Karen collected a load and went out into the rain. She was gone just long enough for Theo to begin to wonder where the child was when she heard her stomping mud off her boots. "I was hunting vots," Karen announced. "I saw a burrow so I went to see how they were doing. And it was empty. Ripped open from the top. And I found another, too. Empty."

"Probably friends of our friend here did it," said Theo. "They must wake up starving."

"Nasty things." Karen picked up four more bags and headed out. "The vots never hurt them when they were helpless."

"Grass feeds the herbivores and herbivores feed the carnivores," said Theo. "A browser feels no sorrow for the grass it eats. This creature feels no sorrow for the browser it eats. Both kill with no malice."

Karen paused to consider this.

"I'm not sure I understand the part about malice yet," she said finally. "Or if I want to. Are there predators among people too?"

Theo paused in her work, wondering if Karen was thinking of her parents' death and trying to fit this reason to an acceptance of that loss. If so, it was no time to tell a comforting lie.

"They could be called that, I suppose, those people who inflict great personal harm on others. I would not give them the dignity of calling them predators, but then that is my own prejudice. There is malice in humans; some of us get tainted by our own weakness. . . ."

"Like the people who killed . . ." Karen still could not say it. ". . . who mutinied at Base One?"

"Like them. But for every person who becomes a 'predator' there are a thousand who do not." And then she added, thinking of Karen, "And if we are lucky, there may be one who is really something special."

"You aren't disappointed because that makes me sick?" Karen gestured at the carcass.

"No. It makes me sick too. But, like you, I can shut part of my mind off until it's safe to think again. Now go dump those bags in the freezer before your arms get the shakes from holding them."

Karen studied Theo's face for a moment, but she admitted nothing before turning away. Theo watched her walk out of the tunnel and into daylight.

When Karen returned, she came over to where Theo was working. "If you can stand it, I can," she announced. "What can I do?"

(111)

"If you'll open the bags and hold them out for me, then seal and freeze them, it will save us a lot of time."

"O.K. Are you labeling them?"

"Some of them. I was hoping I'd remember from the film."

"I'll label. We're going to have a lot of sacks."

The work did go much faster with two. The biggest problem was the very size of the creature and Theo's ignorance of it. More than once she wished for a block and tackle and six strong crewmen. Short of that, she used her trusty saw and sent Karen out to the freezer so the girl wouldn't have to watch. By mid-afternoon she had as many tissue samples as she needed. They began to clean up.

It was raining hard now. Karen had the practical idea of simply laying the bloody instruments on the rocks outside. Theo found a bucket in the aircraft and filled it in a puddle to clean up inside. When everything had been packed into the aircraft and they were finished, they were still wearing their rubber suits. Theo's was too messy even to pack into a sealed bag. Nor did she want to smell it when she took her helmet off.

"I'll fix that," Karen yelled above the splatter of rain on their helmets. "You stand there and I'll slosh you off with the bucket."

It seemed like a good idea to Theo until the first bucket of cold water caught her on the stomach. In all the time she had been working she had not gone to the bathroom, not even thought of it. Now, with cold running water all around, she could think of nothing else. She saw Karen scoop up another bucketful and aim at her. With a shrill cry of absolute need, Theo dashed behind the nearest rock. She could hear Karen's laughter above the sound of rain.

(112)

XIX

FOR variety, as Karen said, it was raining in sheets when they took off. Theo radioed the base to report their estimated arrival time. Repeatedly the controller begged her to be careful. "It's raining here too," he said, his voice near tears. Since he knew they were on autopilot, his cautionings appeared excessive.

"What's wrong?" Theo asked. "The rain is a bore, but it's not tragic." There were static and silence until, in response to her repeated calls, the Commander answered. He assured her all was well.

"He didn't talk long," Karen said afterward. "I'd have all kinds of questions I couldn't wait to ask."

"He's very busy with half the staff gone." But it bothered Theo too. The calm Paluvian Commander had sounded harassed.

The clouds made it twilight by four. The last hour they flew in the dark, which really didn't make much difference except psychologically. Both felt relief when the instruments showed they were landing, and they could see the yellow triangle of fog that marked the opening in the hangar dome. Then finally the blue marker lights on the dome slid past the window and they landed with a thump on the wet floor.

Through the window of the aircraft she saw Tairas at the hangar control board. He had the telescopic dome almost closed when she opened the hatch. She released the seat belts. "What do you say to a bath and dinner, Dr. Orlov?"

"I say that is the best idea you've had all day," said Karen. "We skipped lunch. And wisely so." And for that instant Theo wondered which of the girl's parents had said, "and wisely so" in that tone. It seemed a verbal bridge to the past.

"Everything go all right?" The Commander stuck his head through the hatch. They got up to meet him.

"Beautifully," said Theo. "Wait until you see the films."

He sniffed the air and grimaced. ". . . Uh, yes. What exactly did you . . . uh . . . find?"

Theo started to tell him, with Karen's help, but it seemed to the woman he was only half listening. Interested, yes, but . . . "At any rate, our enemy is an exotic predator. Once I get some time in the lab, I can tell you more."

He nodded distractedly and flicked on his wrist intercom. "Crewmen to the hangar to unload the work wagon." Then,

(114)

looking over the dripping hull, "Muddy up there . . . we'll leave the mesh on this car. Just in case we have to go . . . hunting. . . ." He met her questioning look and attempted to smile. "I am very glad you two are back. It is so dark out there . . . so black and empty . . . God!"

Theo caught Karen's eye. Both of them had heard this tone before, but never from this man. Jonathan Tairas was fighting an anxiety attack. Suddenly Theo felt very tired. She put a reassuring hand on Karen's arm.

"Is the whole staff frightened again, Commander?" she said. "Is that what's wrong?"

He made an attempt to regain self-control. "Forgive me. It's like malaria . . . it sneaks up on you. To answer your question, no, not all of us. Only four had to be sedated. Dr. Wexler seems to feel safe. And Philip Park, and the three from the ringworlds. The rest of us are managing. But it is enervating."

"Did you learn something terrible while we were gone? Everyone seemed O.K. this morning."

He shook his head. "Maybe the isolation . . . the rain. You two left us. . . . No. No news really. We made voice contact with the people at Ag. They are all well but frightened, too. I regretted having to tell them about the . . . uh . . . what do you call them? Cave bears? It really put a panic into them. Commander Kim can't reach Base One either. We both agreed to start transmitting a distress signal . . . to space. I have done so. . . ."

He looked as if he were going to express more doubts and saw Karen watching him, her face a mixture of clinical interest and sympathy. He straightened. "But we'll get through this. It's a matter of self-discipline. Now"—his tone became lighter—"forgive my saying so, but you two need a bath. I must not detain you any longer. Believe me!"

The two of them walked through the rain to the living dome, rather than take the new igloo-like passageway. Theo thought they would make a less memorable entrance if they let the rain scrub them a bit more. All the outside lights were on yellow for the fog. Although there were supposed to be armed guards on duty, they saw no one. But the fog was very thick. The only sounds were those of the waves pounding against the rocks.

The lobby fountain was playing soothing lighting music when they entered the dome. The lobby was empty. Along the curving hallway privacy screens were drawn everywhere until they came to Dr. Wexler's room. Theo slowed.

"Let's tiptoe," she whispered. "I don't want her to see me like this. She'll lecture me about personal appearance."

"Maybe she's not in there," whispered Karen.

"Theo Leslie, is that you?" Dr. Wexler appeared in her doorway. "I'm so glad you're back! I was worried—you two are a mess! A positive mess! Or I should say negative mess. When we don't look our best we tend to get ill more . . ."

"Later, Evelyn." As she passed the door, Theo thrust her sleeve under the other woman's nose.

". . . more quickly," Evelyn continued. "You must . . ." The scent came through to her then and a look of such revulsion came over her face that both Karen and Theo burst into laughter. "What *is* that? That is the most wretched . . ."

Still laughing, Theo broke into a run. "Race you to the showers," she called, and Karen passed her.

They dropped their clothes into the laser-fired disposal and bathed with disinfectant, then stood beneath the sunlights for ten minutes and bathed again with perfumed soap and shampoo.

"Do you suppose we're O.K. now?" Karen said finally. "I'm tired of water. And I'm very hungry."

Theo handed her a towel. "We'll go get some robes and I'll drop this off in the Commander's office."

She had forgotten to return the gun to him at the hangar. It was now on the mirror shelf with her watch and belt. But the Commander's office was locked when they passed, and they weren't dressed to go looking for him. Back in their rooms, Theo tossed the gun on her bed, saying, "I'll give it to him later."

Karen was ready first. She stood looking out the window, politely hiding her impatience with Theo's need to blow-dry her hair and make it presentable. Theo could see girl and window reflected in the mirror.

"What is it?" she asked, seeing Karen frown.

"I don't know . . . do you think yellow lights are a good idea?"

"Fog lights? The color penetrates more, I guess. Why?"

"Remember how the animals liked our yellow tent?"

Their eyes met in the mirror. Theo did remember. She knew what Karen meant, and knew why she was getting goose bumps. "You're thinking of the animal that licked the roof? The big eye that shone in the distance?"

Karen nodded. Without a word Theo got up and hooked the gun belt on beneath her robe, then sat down and finished drying her hair.

"I'm going to tell the Commander about the yellow," Karen said and went out to the hall intercom. After a few minutes she

(117)

came back. "He says the automatic guard lasers will stop anything and the white lights glare too much and the alarm will go off and not to worry."

"Good. Let's go eat." Theo wore the weapon to dinner.

XX

THEY found most of the remaining staff in the rec room having dinner. The room was busy with the scent of hot food and chatter. While the tone was not joyous, neither was it as morose as Theo had seen it before. She and Karen were greeted warmly. Their return seemed to cheer the group.

"It's your new image as a mother," Evelyn murmured as they stood waiting for their turn at the servers. "Most of us feel so desperately alone here now that your relationship is very reassuring. . . ."

"That's twaddle, Evelyn!" said Theo.

Karen, who had missed Evelyn's remark, looked up, puzzled. The psychiatrist gave Theo a maddeningly superior smile as a young man passed and patted Karen on the shoulder as one would pat a mascot. "No. It's not. But we won't argue. . . ."

"Hey, Theo. Tell us what you found." The questions began and continued until their food was ready and they sat down at a table.

"You can see the films tomorrow," Dr. Wexler promised them. "Now if you'll excuse us, I have a medical problem to discuss with these two."

"What problem?" Theo smiled up at Philip, who dropped two cubes of wine on their table as he passed.

"Do you see anything psychologically significant in the fact that neither of you suffer from fear?" Evelyn leaned close, as if they were fellow conspirators. Karen drew back and made a face.

"Evelyn. It's been a long, hard day. We're in no mood for analytical discussions. Especially not over dinner. What's your point?" Theo's obvious irritation went ignored by the other woman.

"I find it interesting that some of us seem to be immune. I wonder what it is in our psychological make-up that gives us that extra sense of security?"

"Something obviously makes us superior," Theo quipped, then turned serious. *"Everything* does not have to be mental." She opened her wine canister and took an approving sip. "For all we know this fear is a symptom of something else—a poison we're ingesting from the water perhaps—or the air? Some tiny trace mineral . . ." She paused, something nagging in a corner of her mind. Then Evelyn spoke and the idea was gone.

"It's psychosomatic and you know it. You always feel this need to defend people."

"I always feel the need not to have our privacy totally invaded.

You like to dissect minds and pin them out for study. The best part is destroyed in the operation. I find that perverse."

"Can we eat now?" Karen had been waiting politely for the adults to begin.

"Oh, I—think so," Theo paused as Dr. Wexler abruptly got up from the table. She looked hurt, and Theo felt a pang of remorse at her use of the word "perverse." That must have hit Evelyn right in her self-image.

Theo reached out and caught her by the hand. "Let's talk in the morning."

"If you wish," said Evelyn and departed, all wounded dignity.

Karen watched her go and frowned to herself, then shrugged and dug into her pseudo-chicken tetrazzini.

"Dr. Wexler's hands are damp and icy, and her pulse is fast," said Theo quietly.

"She's scared, too?"

Theo nodded. "But she's keeping it to herself." Then, thinking of her own insensitivity, she added, "Damn!"

"Is it a disease, Theo?"

"The fear? Perhaps in a metaphysical sense—"

"Simon—my father—said that it was like a disease, and tonight the Commander said something like that. And you said maybe a poison or trace mineral."

Theo thought it over as she ate. "They've done all sorts of blood tests, radiation tests, every other kind of test. Nothing." She passed a cube of milk to Karen, who shook her head. Theo put the milk back. "But also, we don't know what to look for. . . ."

The light and music in the room went dim, then hesitantly returned to full power. Under normal conditions no one would

(121)

have paid any attention to a thing like that. But now it produced an outcry of fear. At the next table one man promptly fainted, a woman slid under the table and cowered there, her eyes mad with terror. Several people rushed from the room, bruising themselves against furniture in their panic to escape. "Get the guns! Where are the guns?" someone asked.

It was pitiful to see, Theo thought. These normally highly competent people were almost incapacitated. "It's all right," she called out. "It's all right. You are all still safe. It was a temporary power loss. Nothing bad." Then, appealing to their rational minds, she asked, "What do we have running that would draw like that?"

"The security system, but no alarm went off," Philip Park called from the far side of the room. "Dr. Leslie's right. Relax."

"You can talk," someone muttered. "You don't know."

The noise level returned to normal.

Theo went back to her original train of thought. Evelyn was right; what *was* different about her, Karen, possibly Philip, and the few others who never seemed affected? Had comparative tests been run on the blood of the local animals? Could they be? Their chemical composition was so different. . . .

She realized that Karen had finished eating and was sitting quietly watching people and that she had not spoken for minutes. "I'm sorry," Theo said. "I was thinking."

"I know. Anything?"

"No."

"Want some chocolate cake?"

The lights flickered again while they were walking back to their room. "I wish we could see out," said Karen. As in the rec

(122)

room, an interior space, there were no windows in the tubelike corridor. "I think something's out there."

"Why?"

"When the music's soft . . . listen." Karen stopped still. Faintly above the melody Theo heard a surge of sound.

"That's the waves."

Karen shook her head. "Too high-pitched."

It occurred to Theo that Karen's ears could still hear sounds an adult could not. "Hum what you hear."

The girl attempted a sound starting below low D and arcing up until she coughed.

"I can't go that high—or whir in my throat like that."

They were passing the empty dining room. "Let's look out these windows. We can see better." Karen hesitated a bit but followed Theo in.

The big room was very dark and smelled of damp carpet and disinfectant. With the privacy curtain shut, the hall noises were inaudible. Rain drummed steadily on the dome. The new window was a yellow oblong of fog and water drops sparkling from the fog lights outside. They stood by the window, peering into the murk.

"There! Where the fog moved! . . ."

"What?"

"Something . . . there! See it?"

For a second Theo saw a dim bulk, perhaps brown, at the limit of light penetration. The fog blew shut again.

"What do you think?"

"Could be a browser—one of the big swamp creatures?"

"How far is the swamp?"

"Maybe a hundred miles down the coast," admitted Theo. Karen didn't voice her doubt on that speculation. She didn't have to. They stood close in silence for a long time. Finally Theo said, "Let's go to bed."

Just as they turned to go, something out there screamed. The sound cut through all other sounds and, when it ended, seemed to have purchased total silence. The warble alarm began to make loops of sound.

XXI

POWERFUL lasers were firing. A more secure defense system had been rigged into the base power grid. Something had crossed a boundary out there in the fog, tripped a wire or broken a light beam. All dome lights went dim; the music went off.

Theo heard the distinct "Pmmp! pmmp!" of the weapon's pulsing. The animal cried out again in agony. In her mind she imagined its pain, and her body involuntarily writhed in empathy.

"There are two—three! Of them!" Karen pointed.

Air currents were moving, generated by the big animals themselves or the intense heat of the weapons, shifting the fog. For perhaps thirty seconds they could see the creatures. The largest, the one in the line of fire, lay on the ground, its eyes wild, its body jolted by each pulse of the laser. Behind the dying creature were two more, both tugging with mouth, claws, and front legs to pull the victim away.

"Are they going to eat it?" Karen whispered.

"No . . ." Theo hesitated. "I *think* they are trying to help it."

"Oh-h! They're intelligent?"

"Watch them."

"I don't want to. That's sad." But she did. She saw them pull the fallen animal free and tug it away, out of the misty light. The laser shut off. The fog swirled in. From beyond the light came one more cry. Then quiet.

Guards ran past the window on the path below. As full power returned, the music swelled up. In the hallway voices called out. Theo heard it all and yet did not, thinking about that last noise from the creatures. Was it a cry of terminal pain or of grief for a fallen comrade?

"What can they do for it?" Karen asked as they crossed the room.

"Nothing," Theo was going to say and then did not; that was too hopeless an answer. "They can at least comfort each other." She gave Karen's shoulders a little squeeze. "Come on. Let's go join our fellow animals. I'm sure they need a little comforting too." She opened the curtains into the hall.

"Attention. Attention," ordered the Commander's voice on the intercom. "We have had some excitement outside. No one has been hurt. In the fog animals ran into the security wires and tripped off the lasers. One animal was wounded, but it has gone. I repeat, none of our staff was hurt. So please, relax. Go back to what you were doing."

(126)

"Did *he* see what happened?" Karen said.

"He doesn't want to frighten people."

"There they are," someone called, "coming out of the dining room."

The hall was suddenly full of staff.

"They were in *there?*" Evelyn came running out of Theo's room and saw them. "How could you go in there?" And without waiting to be answered, "Did you see anything? Is this dome being attacked? I was afraid you went outside. I was looking—"

"Shhh!" hissed Theo, and grinned at her. "Shush! Yes, we saw something. We saw mostly fog and the laser beams cutting through it. They hit what we think was one of the cave bears. But we couldn't be sure." She looked at the faces around her, all worried, all seeking reassurance, and understood Tairas's attitude.

"Do you think there are others, Theo?" The speaker was the staff cartographer.

"Yes." She would not lie. "But I also think the lasers will kill any animal that crosses the line. No more will try tonight."

"How can you be sure?" asked Philip.

"I can't be. But they . . . animals quickly learn to avoid things that cause death to a fellow animal. As we quickly learned, these animals were dangerous to us, and we took steps to avoid direct contact with them."

"In a minute she's going to give us her famous 'they would eat you with no malice' speech," said Evelyn, who had obviously recovered some semblance of composure. "I have never found it comforting."

"But it's true!" said Karen in defense of her friend.

(127)

"Possibly, but still not comforting, O True Believer," said Evelyn. "I can see you two are going to get along."

"Yes," agreed Theo, "we do. And will. But as I was saying, don't waste sleep waiting for the alarm to go off again. I think we're safe. Besides, half of us have guard duty in some form or other and we need our rest." Although, considering their state of mind, what good some of them would be on guard duty was debatable.

When, an hour or so later, she left them in the lounge and she and Karen went off to bed, she asked Control to "waken A-7 at seven a.m."

"How come we have to get up so early?" yawned Karen.

"You don't. I'm going to follow any tracks I can find as soon as it's daylight."

"Can I go along?"

"Might not be worth getting up for," said Theo.

It surprised neither of them when Karen was awake before the bell tone the next morning. It was barely light outside. They met Tairas having breakfast in the lounge. He looked bleary-eyed, but he was clean-shaven. "To celebrate," he said. "I wasn't sure our line of defense would hold against those things. It was such a relief to know it does."

"Did they find a body?" Theo asked.

"Just tracks. I think the thing walked away. But to survive a blast like . . ." He saw Karen shaking her head. "What?"

"The other two dragged it off," she whispered so that the other staff could not hear and be frightened. "We saw them."

"You're not serious?"

"Yes," Theo said. "We're going out and track them."

(128)

"I'm going with you," he said.

They drove a land cruiser, the surface equivalent of the utility craft. It was a sturdy car with fat tires and inadequate suspension for a world without roads. Every crew who ever used them immediately referred to them as "bouncers."

The ground was so torn up at the spot where the animal had hit the wire that the rain had washed away all tracks. Water filled a long depression leading away from the base. Theo rode with her head out the open door, watching the ground. At several spots along the drag path she saw sets of deep claw indentations.

The trail led up through the trees and out into the rolling foothills that lay between sea and mountains. Where grass grew, the track was easy to follow. When it reached a lumpy hillside of rock outcropping, they lost it. They circled back and forth for half an hour. The trail ended on the loose rock. Tairas stopped the car and they sat there, at a loss about where to look next.

Karen jumped out to look at some flowers growing among the rocks. A child of new worlds, she looked but did not touch, admired color but did not sniff their scent. A flower could be harmless, or cause a mild rash, or induce death. One rule held: the more color, the more danger. These looked like bright orange artichokes with red bristles.

Something else caught her attention. Theo watched the girl splash up over the rocks, head down, hands clasped behind her yellow slicker. She stopped midway on the slope and stood looking at the ground, then turned and waved for them to join her.

"What is it?" Tairas called. "Did you find a track?"

Karen just pointed. The two adults got out and walked up the slope in the rain. Once they reached her, it took a little time

(129)

for them to see what she was pointing at. Then Theo noticed that the surface of the rocks appeared to be moving. She stepped closer. It was a swarm of meat pudding creatures.

"What are those?" Tairas's lip curled.

"Scavengers," Theo said. "I saw one before, up where you met us. They evidently come out with the rain."

"Revolting!"

"I thought so."

The rocks were covered with them, all active, all scuttling about. Wet brown bags of skin and legs, going under the rocks and emerging again endlessly.

"What are they feeding on?" said Tairas, and as he said it, they all could guess.

"It's there!" they chorused together and then laughed. Theo's laugh broke off. "Who buried it? Who covered it with stone?"

"Its friends?" suggested Karen, and Theo believed her.

XXII

RAIN. Day after night after day of rain. The domes developed leaks in odd places and had to be repaired. A heating and de-humidifying system had to be devised. Drainage ditches were dug around the domes. The monotony of the rain was equaled only by the work it created.

The corporate rule of "no excess" on expeditions applied to the number of personnel, as well as everything else. With half the staff gone, those remaining would have been busy in normal cir-cumstances. Now a fourteen-hour day was a light work load. But, in a way, the extra work was a blessing. It kept people from having time to think.

There were no more attacks on the dome. Sometimes, in the

mornings, there would be tracks of the creatures in the mud by the lake, and deep prints on the hill behind the base, as if the animals stood up there in the rain at night, watching. But no person dared to go up there at night to see.

Theo spent most of her days in the lab. With the discovery of the creature's burial, Tairas suspected they were dealing with an intelligent life form. He had returned with a crew and excavated the site. The scavengers had left little, even in so short a time, but still clasped in the right foreclaws of the skeleton had been two large crystals. The sight of them there had so frightened him, he privately confessed later to Theo, that he had looked around, expecting to see the victim's fellows come running to avenge this desecration. He had ordered the grave closed and returned to its original condition.

"The position of the crystals may be accidental," Theo told him. "The act of burying a fallen comrade instinctive. I suspect they bury one another when they collapse from dehydration. It is a mistake to read human feeling into the actions of other animals." She smiled. "Besides, if we believe them capable of reason, it will scare everybody silly."

"What do you believe, Theo?"

"Nothing, yet. You can't begin to know any creature until you've studied it at ease in its own environment. The lab will give us bits and pieces of fact—but not the living thing."

"I want to know the relationship between creature and crystals," he said.

So she set to work on the crystals, even though they were what interested her least about the animal. What she wanted to study was cryptobiosis. One important discovery had been made. There

(132)

was in the lab an "Eridan chamber," a plastic tank in which the normal desert-like conditions of the planet were duplicated so that small specimens could be kept alive and studied at close range. Karen had brought in one of the meat puddings and released it into the chamber. It immediately lost its appetite and began to shrink. In three days it resembled a buffalo chip. When put into a bell jar with sand and with humidity rising gradually over a ten-hour period, it swelled and returned to life and apparent good health.

Later, on the basis of this and subsequent experiments, under Theo's guidance, Karen wrote her first published paper, "The Cryptobiotic Characteristics of Specific Cephalopodic Scavengers on Eridan."

Karen's simple experiments promised excitement with the big animal. But there would be time for that later. First the crystals. Where was the base file on them?

Both of the Expedition's experts on crystals were dead; Joan Lee and Genis Illian, geologists. "Why didn't they go with the others to hunt crystals that day?" she wondered aloud as she waited for the computer to retrieve their notes. "Did they have other duties that prevented it? Or weren't they interested? If the crystals are so valuable, why would the two people most likely to know where to find the best specimens stay in camp?"

"Maybe they had their weight limit already?" Karen was stretched out on the lounge under the window, reading.

"Maybe. But everybody else keeps on looking for bigger and better ones." The bell dinged on her terminal, indicating the retrieval of printed matter. She turned her attention to the screen.

The geologists' report gave the chemical composition of the

(133)

crystals and identified them as proteins, "infinite numbers of small protein crystallites mixed with foreign substances." It speculated on their growth in a gel-like media, marveled at their alignment, hardness, and insolubility. It concluded by noting the crystals were "of great curiosity and worthy of extended study. Gem value: None. Commercial value: To be determined."

"Hasn't anybody read this?" was Theo's first reaction, then remembered that she had not bothered to read it. She had had no interest in the stones, other than aesthetic appreciation. But the others? She pushed the cross-index key, and Illian's face appeared on the screen, speaking in his soft Russian accent.

"As a matter of permanent record, Dr. Lee and I are aware of the rumored value of these crystals. The rumor apparently originated at Base One. It is said our analyses were falsified to protect Corporate interests or to avoid gold fever. This is untrue. These crystals are not of geologic origin or of known mineral values. They are organics, and unique. With research, biochemists may find a use for them. We know of none presently. Dr. Lee and I have found our facts ignored, and we lack the time to defend our findings constantly." Illian's image smiled. "It would be ironic if, considering the esteem in which these crystals are held, they turned out to be gravel from the renal systems of the local beasts. In any event, collecting them is a harmless pastime for the crew."

Hearing this, Karen began to grin. "The crystals are worthless? All this fuss and they're worthless!"

Theo didn't answer. Karen looked over to see if she had said something out of order. One glance and she knew Theo had heard nothing she said. The woman sat staring at the screen, her eyes narrowed in concentration, pupils moving slightly as thoughts came and went, lips open over precisely clenched teeth, respiration shallow. It was familiar; the look of the fanatic, the totally absorbed. Karen sighed, but silently so she wouldn't distract.

Theo slipped off the stool and went to rummage through the samples they had brought back from the cave. "Protein?" She repeated the word twice. "What kind of protein? What form . . . ?" She extracted a small vial containing one of the crystals and brought it back to the workbench. Then, as if on impulse, she put it into the isolation chamber, opened the vial with the mechanical hands, and prepared a sample for the electron microscope.

Karen went back to her book. An hour passed, then two. She looked up once to see Theo taking blood samples from her own finger and watched her face as she studied them under the microscope. Then saw her smile to herself with satisfaction. But she made no comment. Karen went back to her book.

When she heard Theo approach the sofa, Karen merely held out her hand. Theo smiled down at her as she sterilized and punctured the girl's index finger. "Evelyn's right," she said, "we are a good match. Squeeze." With Karen pressing the disinfectant pad on the wounded finger, Theo retreated with her sample.

Again and again the microscope hummed to itself. The lights came on outside as night fell. Karen's stomach began to growl. At last she heard Theo turn off the equipment.

"It's a virus," she said. "The crystal is a virus colony."

Karen tried to understand this. From Theo's tone, it was obviously important. But the girl could not pretend. "What does that mean?" she said.

(135)

"I *think* it means your father and Tairas were on the right track. I think this fear is a symptom of viral infection. And you and I have either a natural immunity to it, or we were lucky enough to get a mild dose and immunized ourselves."

"When I tasted it!"

"Maybe. I don't know. I tasted it too. And then we left them alone."

Karen thought it over. "You know," she said, "we are either very smart or very simple. But lucky."

"Lucky, I think. Want to see why?"

XXIII

THE microscope's film showed a tiny hexagonal shape floating in the fluid between the blood cells. Seemingly at random, it glided to rest upon a cell's surface.

"What's it doing?" said Karen.

"Drilling. It sends a pipe down through the cell wall. Into the pipe it secretes a substance, a nucleic acid, that makes the host cell reproduce more virus. The new virus moves out and attacks other cells. This virus doesn't kill the host cell. It simply takes it over."

"It's a vampire!" said Karen. "It bites the cell's neck and makes it one of the living dead! It forces it to do evil things . . ." She saw the look on Theo's face and sputtered to a halt. ". . . Well, it is. Sort of?"

Theo grinned. "Yes. Sort of. Where did you learn about vampires?"

"On Coreco. Where I shot roaches. It's a mining planet. Very dull. There's a big library on the base. Nobody used the library much, but I liked it. They had a lot of great books. How come this virus doesn't make our animal sick?"

Theo sorted through and chose to reply to the question. "I don't know. Maybe because the cave bears are immune. Maybe because the animal's system segregates the virus and renders it harmless. Or the virus may be beneficial to them, even essential. They seem to cherish the crystals. . . . When the animal goes into its cryptobiotic state, the virus may follow suit. It may be expelled from muscle or nerve tissue and congregate in the renal system, as Illian suggests." Theo paused to speculate on that, then shrugged. "I don't know, Karen."

"So what are you going to do?"

"Tell the Commander what we've found. Then turn it over to Evelyn and her medical staff—all four of them—they are the experts in this field. I wonder how long it takes to find an antibody?" She glanced at her watch as if considering starting that now.

"Let's eat before you do anything else, O.K.?"

On their way out they passed the bell jar where a revived meat pudding scuttled about, searching for escape. "That thing must be full of bugs!" said Karen.

Theo stopped and stared down at it. "I wonder if it is . . . and how it . . ." Karen pulled her out the door.

Their dinner was delayed. En route Theo stopped off at the

Commander's office. After listening to her for a few minutes, he wanted to come back to the lab and see for himself.

"If it's hard enough to be a crystal, how are our people getting contaminated? If they are?" he asked.

"By touch. It's acid soluble," Theo said. "Saliva or normal skin acid will do nicely. Each time we handle a crystal, we could be reinfecting ourselves."

Tairas stared at the crystal fragment glowing in the isolation chamber. "I've seen people spit-polishing them," he mused to himself. ". . . Damn! Why didn't I read that report!"

Armed with the geologists' report and Theo's findings, he called a staff meeting and presented the facts. He concluded by saying all crystals were to be collected and placed in impermeable bags, sealed and brought to the hangar. From there they would be flown back into the hills and buried.

"So someone else can find them?" protested Felix. "No thanks. I didn't believe the geology report, and I'm not about to take a biologist's word for it. I'm keeping my stones."

There were murmurs of agreement from around the room.

The Commander looked as if he were going to argue, then changed his mind. "Get one of your crystals, Dr. Felix. Bring it to the lab. The rest of us will be there."

Felix hesitated, then went.

In the lab Tairas took the crystal Felix had brought, put it in the isolation chamber, and applied a flame. After a few seconds the "stone" began to burn. There were no more arguments.

As Evelyn said, "We may be greedy, but once we understand the situation, we're not stupid." But even she was surprised by the quantity of supposed gems the staff had managed to collect.

"Four tons!" she told Theo as they worked together in the lab the next morning. "Four tons of dreams! Do you know how it makes people feel to give up something like that? The disappointment . . ."

"I know how it feels to give up a dream," Theo said. "But there is a subtle difference between dream and obsession."

"If *you* don't value it, it's an obsession." Evelyn lost her sarcasm in curiosity. "What dreams have you given up? You never told me about them."

"Nor will I," said Theo. "At least not while we have this much work. Now, do you want me to do blood samples from the staff today, or correlate the stats on the weekly samples?"

"Felix is getting today's batch. You do the correlation."

For the next few days Theo spent almost all her waking time in the medical lab. When she wasn't there she was in her biology lab. She was up before Karen woke and often didn't return until the girl was asleep. She had habitually worked that way, totally absorbed. Content.

She had learned already that those who were immune to the effect of the crystal virus all carried another alien virus in their systems, a virus shared with vots. The vot virus not only was harmless to humans but rendered the crystal virus harmless. With that information the medical staff was working in two directions; a vaccine direct from the crystal virus and an antiviral agent corresponding to the vots' interference phenomenon. Theo favored the vot route, Evelyn the vaccine route. Both were aware of little else.

Then one afternoon Theo looked out the lab window and saw Karen and Philip walking down toward the beach. The rain had stopped; it was beginning to do that now. Sometimes it quit raining for as long as two hours at a stretch. Karen was wearing Theo's favorite beige sweat shirt, and the girl was telling the man something with her usual great enthusiasm, and he was laughing. How nice it was to see enthusiasm for life instead of the restraint or ennui of adults, Theo thought. How good to laugh at . . .

"Why the wistful look?" Evelyn's voice broke into her thoughts. "You are going to miss that child when this is over. In a way, it might be good for you, Theo Leslie, make you more human. You never have been vulnerable where people are concerned. Just animals. But as for Karen . . . you see her missing you now, wearing that big ugly sweat shirt of yours for security. That child—"

"Shut up, Evelyn," said Theo and hurried out of the lab. Damn Evelyn and her constant analyses, she thought as she walked down the hall. Damn the Corporation and their rules. Damn the fools who killed Karen's parents—and damn Evelyn again because she's right! Theo broke into a run to escape to her own room and the luxury of tears.

A half hour alone and she had recovered enough composure to blow her nose, wash her face, brush her hair, and set to work to solve the problem. In the Commander's office was a large volume of corporate law which supposedly covered any legal situation that could possibly arise. It was very definite on the status of juveniles on expedition; none was allowed unless accompanied by one natural parent.

"Orphaned juveniles will be returned to the source of maternal origin, there to become wards of the nearest living relative if said juvenile and relative so mutually desire, or in lieu of this, become a ward of the Corporation and placed in an environment suitable to the ward's intellect and education until said juvenile attains majority." Theo read it, snapped the book shut, put it back on the shelf, and went off to find Jonathan Tairas.

He was in the dome core reloading the automated food service equipment. "Who has this passion for turkey?" he asked when he saw her come in. "Twenty-two cases of turkey dinners!" He shuddered.

"How can I adopt Karen?"

He looked up from his work and was going to make a joke, then saw she was in no mood for it. "I'm not at all sure you can," he said. "The Book says—"

"I just read it."

"Have you discussed it with Karen?"

"No."

He put another stack of trays into the server and aligned them carefully. Too carefully. "You're the third person to express interest in adoption. Karen talked to me about it yesterday. She said she wanted to stay with you. If you wanted her. As you quite obviously do, pale face."

"Why didn't you tell me?"

"Karen asked me not to. She said she knew it was—and I quote —'a great responsibility to know someone loves you and if the person being loved doesn't want to be, very awkward'—unquote. So if you never thought of it yourself, she didn't want you to feel awkward."

"Who else wants to adopt her?"

He gave a wry grin. "Me. Now I feel awkward." And he turned back to the machine to hide his feelings.

"How very dear you can be beneath that reserve of yours," she said impulsively.

"Strange that you should say that, Doctor . . . are you sure you want her, Theo? You've always been a loner. Like me. You're always eager to go off to some godforsaken world like this to study strange beasts. If you could keep her with you, have you thought what it means? The day-to-day living? Now it's fun, because she is precocious and charming—and you met dramatically—you felt sorry for her. But you also know there will be a definite ending to her being with you. If she were your child, she would be with you constantly for at least seven more years. You would be responsible for her through these troublesome years of adolescence—for her education, for her safety, for her happiness. There are so few people out here who are her age. She will rely on you for everything. Friend, mother—suppose you fall in love and she is jealous. Suppose—"

"Jonathan." She called him to a halt. "You've thought of all this and you still want to adopt her. Don't anticipate. You have worked with me on five expeditions. You know me as well as you know any of your staff. You've known Karen through most of her life. You knew her parents. Do you think we will—" She paused and took a deep breath. "I love that child very much. The question is, can I keep her?"

XXIV

With a promise of total support from Tairas, Theo set off to talk to Karen. The girl wasn't in any of the domes. Finally she found Philip, who said he had left her by the ocean. "She said she wanted to do some serious thinking. But that was an hour ago or more."

Theo found her there, hidden by the cliff, on a rock, sitting with her hands clasped around her knees, watching waves the color of weak coffee come smashing in to shore.

With Karen unaware of another human presence, Theo stopped to study her as she would have an unsuspecting animal. In repose Karen's face was no longer childlike, merely young. There was something around the eyes and the taut jawline, a self-contained thing that looked out and analyzed and kept its own private counsel. A gust of wind feathered her hair across her face and she shook it back, then leaned forward and rested her head against her knees, as if suddenly overwhelmed by fatigue—or by being trapped forever in her own skin.

It was a movement so curiously private that Theo felt shame at witnessing it. Not wanting Karen to know she had been spying, she almost ran back up the cliff and walked north until another path led down to the beach. From there Karen could see her coming and present the self she wished to show.

Theo stopped to pick up a curious seashell, spiraled, like a hexagonal orange pagoda with a round hole in its base. She washed the wet sand off it in an incoming wave. When she looked up, Karen was running down the beach to join her.

"How come Evelyn let you out?" she called. "Are you done?"

"I escaped." Theo handed her the shell. "Have a present."

Karen's face lit up as she took it. "It's beautiful." She looked it over thoroughly and fingered the points polished bright by the sand. "I wish we could stay on this world and never had to go someplace else. I wish . . ." She looked up to see Theo's reaction to that wish.

"It is a beautiful world," agreed Theo, wondering how to start the conversation she had come for and suddenly shy. "I talked to Jonathan Tairas today, Karen. I asked him . . . if I could adopt you."

She took three more steps before realizing Karen had stopped. As she turned to see why, the girl engulfed her in a bear hug so vigorous it nearly toppled them both into the sand. "I don't know if I can," Theo cautioned when she could breathe again. "Don't get your hopes up too much. We'll . . ."

"I know! I read the Book! I'm so glad you want me! Evelyn said you were used to . . . well, not having anyone to worry about, and you liked animals four hundred per cent more than people, and I thought maybe you were just being kind to me, and . . ."

"Evelyn told you *that* ?"

"No. Not me. She talks too much but she's not cruel. I was curled up in the chair in the lobby and she didn't see me. She was walking by, talking to someone else. She didn't know I heard."

"O.K.," Theo said carefully. "People love to gossip. Especially in a closed society like ours. You may overhear other things that upset you. There are several important things I want you to hear from me. Just in case you don't know already." She took a deep breath. "I think you are a very special person, Karen Orlov. You are bright and dear and so brave sometimes you nearly break my heart. Whatever the legal ruling is, I want you to know—I love you very much."

Karen's eyes never left hers as Theo spoke. Theo watched her attempt to smile and then saw her chin start to quiver and her eyes well up with tears. She reached out and pulled the girl close into her arms for comfort as she cried.

Karen tried to say something between sobs. Theo couldn't understand a word of it. She was about to murmur placations and then stopped, remembering "there—there—dears" murmured to herself once long ago. "For all I know," Theo thought, "the first sob was relief and all the rest old grief remembered and now

(146)

being accepted." Out of respect for Karen she would not presume to murmur. She lay her cheek against the girl's damp hair and remained silent.

Gradually the sobs diminished, the grip relaxed a little, and she felt Karen's body grow less tense. She freed one arm, reached into her pocket for tissues, and used one to wipe her own tears. As she did so, she wondered at herself. For someone for whom years passed without crying, she was certainly doing a lot of it.

She could hear Evelyn explaining it to her and damned the woman again silently.

"I got your jacket all wet." Karen took the rest of the tissues and blew her nose vigorously.

"That's O.K. I got your head a little damper. We're even." They grinned at each other rather self-consciously.

"Theo?"

"Yes?"

"What I said was, I love you too. Oh." Karen reached up with a tissue. "Your eyes are still leaking." She carefully patted the corners of Theo's eyes. "I think we should walk up the beach awhile, Dr. Leslie. You appear to be having a crying jag."

Theo nodded. "I think you are right, Dr. Orlov. And then we will go get us a good stiff hot chocolate."

Hand in hand, they set off over the wet sand.

(147)

XXV

IT did not rain any more that day. That night no one slept well. It was too quiet. You could hear every noise. And what if that sound out there wasn't the wind but the Animal? Was that the ocean's roar or was it the big aircraft from Base One? And that noise . . . ?

Theo lay wide-eyed in bed, not afraid, just not relaxed. She heard the guards each time they passed her window. There were muffled voices, footpads in the hall. From Karen's alcove came the slow, deep breathing of sleep.

"If I get up, will I wake her? Or if she wakens after I'm gone, will she be frightened?" she thought, then smiled at her own worrying and slipped out of bed. But stealthily. In the lit bathroom she wrote a note, "Went to lab. Back soon. Go to sleep," laid it on her pillow, and slipped out into the night-lit hall.

Maybe ten people were in the rec room when she passed, some watching a movie, others lulled to sleep by the noise of the sound track. Felix was doing his laundry in the sonic cleaner. He waved a pair of socks at her as she passed. Tairas's door was open. She glanced in and saw him stretched out across his bed, fully dressed, snoring in exhaustion. She paused to close his privacy screen.

Someone had left all the lights on in the medical lab. She reached out and shut them off.

"Hey! Who did that?" Evelyn called from a corner.

"Me."

"Why aren't you in bed?"

"Why aren't you?"

"Because . . . If you really want to know, I came down to run a blood test. I feel abnormally confident tonight, and I wanted to see if it was physical or mental."

Theo smiled. "Don't trust yourself when you feel normal these days, huh?"

"No," Evelyn said bluntly. "Neither would you if . . . but I'm glad you don't know what this fear is like, Theo. It's terrible. There's been nothing that doesn't frighten me. I've been afraid in my bathroom—the closed screen gives me acute claustrophobia. I'm afraid of anything sharp. Darkness. Swimming. Flying. Too many people in a room. I'm afraid I'm going to die." She paused. "In a way it's been very educational. I never knew before what some patients suffered. Of course there's no antibody for it, normally. . . ."

(149)

"Are you telling me you have one?" said Theo.

"Not an antibody. An interferon. None of ours worked. I—uh —extracted the interferon from your blood. And injected myself."

"What is an interferon?"

"Exactly what the name suggests. A chemical substance that interferes with and prevents harmful virus from attacking cells."

"You played guinea pig?"

"I had nothing to lose, Theo. I was so scared I had to fight the thought of suicide. I didn't want to waste time with rats. And the vaccine will take weeks—" The green light came on in the keyboard. She reached up to touch it, then hesitated, "If it shows my virus count isn't down, will I get scared again, Theo?"

"Aren't you sure it's the virus that causes the fear?"

"That's what I'm afraid of now," said Evelyn and made herself laugh. "That it isn't a viral infection. What if we're afraid because we know too much, because we've traveled too far, because there's no place that's home and it is beginning to occur to all of us that we are mortal and of no more importance than a meteor? There is no cure for that—"

"You mean we're all human?" Theo said and simultaneously reached over and touched the green button.

She saw Evelyn recoil like a dog that has been kicked, and her first instinct was to comfort her as she would have Karen. But common sense warned her that sympathy would be no favor; it would merely weaken the woman's already threatened reserve of strength. She let her hand come to rest casually on Evelyn's right shoulder. "Let's look at your blood test first. We can fuss later."

"I don't think I can look."

(150)

"Yes, you can," Theo assured her. "Every symptom is not psychosomatic, Evelyn. Something about this virus is affecting human neurotransmitters. It is scrambling the message from one nerve to the next. Just because you can't isolate which chemicals are involved, or how it works, does not mean it's not happening. You know that. We need expertise and five years of study. In the meantime, let's look and see if the vot virus will control it."

Two test slides were viewed side by side; one was peppered with tiny dark spots; the other showed less than half as many.

"It's working!" she heard Evelyn whisper. "See the fluorescent spots?" Evelyn touched more buttons and the picture on the left changed. "I took the test interferon thirty-six hours ago. That's my blood sample taken three hours later . . ."

"Did anyone ever tell you you have lovely type-B negative?"

"Oh, yes. I was the family beauty, you know. See, at eighteen hours it's beginning to be noticeable." Evelyn turned and grasped Theo's wrist. "Can you spare a pint?"

"Sure. But now? It's two a.m."

"You can sleep while you're doing it."

Theo shrugged. "Why not? You can have more if you like."

"No. That's all I need. Now. Was Felix still up when you came in? I'm going to need some help."

"I can help you."

"No. You're going to bed when I'm done with you."

"But I was going to work on my cave bear tissues."

"Not tonight." Totally her confident self again, Evelyn rose from the terminal and led Theo to the nearest work table. "Up," she ordered. "I can plug you in here." She rummaged through a drawer in the table. "Where are those blood-pacs? Good!"

(151)

With expert hands, she inserted the needle painlessly into Theo's arm and watched the tube begin to fill. "Good. Good." Theo thought of Karen's vampires and giggled.

Half an hour later she had had her sugary drink as a reward and was sent off to bed. Evelyn and Felix were busy at the centrifuge and hardly aware when Theo went. As she stepped out into the hall, she saw the light switch, and thought to herself that next time she saw lab lights on, she would mind her own business.

The note was still on her pillow, but a line had been added. It said, "O.K., but I don't like it." She glanced over at the alcove. Karen was again sound asleep.

Once in her own bed with the covers pulled up, she started to think about Evelyn's success, how happy it would make the crew. A light rain was beginning to fall. It was the last sound she heard for eight hours.

XXVI

SHE woke to the click of a tray being placed on the desk. There was a bounce as someone sat on the end of her bed. A familiar hand clasped her left foot.

"Hmm?"

"Dr. Wexler said to wake you before you got a headache from too much sleep. Besides, you've already missed the sun."

"It was out?" Theo opened one eye and gave her a groggy smile. "Good morning."

"Good morning." Karen tilted her head to check more closely. "Are you really awake, Theo, or are you being pleasant and hoping I'll go away again for an hour? Because if you're awake I'll tell you what's happening, but if you're not I won't."

Theo closed her eye and thought that over. "I think I'm awake," she decided. "Can I listen with my eyes shut?"

"O.K. You have a pillow wrinkle line over your nose and down your cheek."

"Does it add distinction to my character?"

"No. It just looks like somebody folded you wrong."

Theo laughed and sat up. "You win, I'm awake."

Karen slid off the bed and handed her the glass of juice. "Just so you don't fall asleep again."

Theo obediently drank. "How long was the sun out?"

"Almost an hour! I saw three weejees—little ones—they are so dear! And flocks of fliers are going north, above the clouds." She pointed to the rain-streaked window. "It's just drizzling now."

"Any sign of our cave bears last night?"

"No. Dr. Wexler said when you had breakfast, could you come to her lab?"

Theo smiled. "And I thought she was worried about my getting a headache from oversleeping. How did she look to you this morning, by the way?"

Karen thought for a minute. "Pretty messy. But her eyes are— I don't know. It's like this morning she was really smiling and before it was always pretend. I don't think she's afraid any more. Just very tired."

"I think you're right, Dr. Orlov. That's how she hit me last night." She told Karen what had gone on in the lab the night before.

(154)

"That's why she wants you to run tests on our—" Karen began.

"Attention! Attention!" The intercom in the hall came on full volume and so unexpectedly that both of them jumped. The speaker's voice was strange.

"Bother!" whispered Theo. "I'm not even showered or dressed." She had one foot on the carpet when the voice repeated, "Attention! Attention! Eridan Base Three. This is the Aurora Corporation flagship *Prince Vladimir,* responding to your S.O.S. Vice Regent Koh in command. Respond on channel blue. Respond on channel blue."

"Vice Regent Koh?" Karen asked confirmation in a worried whisper. Theo nodded yes. "She's from Palus," said Karen.

"Isn't everyone who matters?" said Theo and began to brush her hair hurriedly. "Have you met her?"

"No. Why are you doing that? The ship's probably a week out. Nobody can see you"

"Attention! Attention! Eridan Base Three, this is—"

"*Vladimir,* this is Eridan Base Three. Base Commander Tairas responding. And grateful to hear your voice. But please lower your transmission. You're coming in on everything that isn't plastic."

"Eridan Base Three. Give your identifying code."

A series of high-frequency tones began repeating sequentially.

"Acknowledged, Commander Tairas. We are going to attempt video . . . we have a picture . . . glitching . . . but adequate. . . ." There was a rasp of deafening static.

"Lower your transmission," Tairas's voice repeated.

(155)

"Sorry." The hall speaker fell silent.

Theo sighed as if released from enthrallment. "I must get dressed. I must get to work. I must . . ." She stopped and looked at Karen sitting on the bed. Three months ago on the trip out here she must have seen this girl on the ship a dozen times and never gave her a passing thought. Nor had Karen given her one. Three months from now would they be strangers again? And would time seem so empty as she was suddenly afraid it would?

"The Vice Regent will decide what happens to us—all of us, the Expedition . . ."

"Yes." Karen seemed to be half listening. "She's a great-aunt of my mother's. She's impressed by two things, money and intelligence. She put up Palus's share of the Corporation. . . ."

"How do you know this?"

"I listen. People think children don't hear them when they talk business. But I did." She got up quickly. "I'm going to the lab, Theo. I want to work on my meat pudding. See you." And she was gone, leaving Theo to stare after her, perplexed. What was so important about meat puddings that it came before curiosity about the approaching flagship?

But as she dressed she thought of all the things that should be done before that ship arrived. First of all, she had to file a petition to adopt, along with character references. There were preliminary studies to do on a dozen different specimens. There was the work on cryptobiosis; Evelyn's group might need considerable help, and she was one of the few remaining people among the small staff who could truly help them. She wanted time to go back out into the field when the rains ended, to observe the dehydration of these creatures. Was cryptobiosis common among Eridan's creatures? And—

"Attention. Attention," the Commander's voice requested. "Would all available staff not on guard duty please report to communications ASAP? The Corporation wants a candid look at you."

XXVII

FIVE days later the *Prince Vladimir* entered Eridan's orbit. From the surface of the planet the ship was visible each dawn. It glowed in the southern sky like a stray comet or a transient morning star. Or hope, Theo thought as she looked at it.

The sky was lighting behind the layered clouds, turning them the bruised reds and purples of this world. The sea was dark brown and noisy with high tide. Wind pushed clouds across that patch of open sky where the starship gleamed. The ship winked in the rising sun's rays and then was obscured by mist. Theo shivered as if she had seen a bad omen.

She had risen early, as had always been her habit. There was to her a sense of continuity about the hour of dawn. It gave her a sense of quietness, purity, an intimacy with the real life of that particular world on which she walked. As there was on the Earth of her childhood; as there had been on a dozen different worlds, as existed here on Eridan, so would there be dawns on worlds to come. Forever and ever. Amen.

But the magic was missing from this dawn. In fact it had been missing since the *Vladimir* spoke. With that strange voice a tight knot seemed to have settled around her midsection. The knot diminished her appetite, made her sleep fitfully, and caused her to be accused of prolonged staring into space.

"What's wrong with me?" she wondered. "Have I given up hope? Did it go when Karen said, 'She's from Palus'? And why does it matter so much to me, the thought of never seeing this child again? Why physical pain?"

Karen was worrying, too. It was nothing she said but what she avoided saying by spending almost all her time working on her meat pudding study. She was data-researching subjects far beyond her. Theo helped her, almost as if it were a game both played to pass the time.

But at night Karen ground her teeth in her sleep and moaned in bad dreams. The first time she slipped from her bed and hurried to the alcove, Theo's impulse had been to put her arms around this lost creature and comfort her. But then she paused, remembering her own recent dreams. Where Karen's mind was at that moment, Theo Leslie had not been, did not exist. So she turned on a soft light and knelt to call the girl back to the present. When Karen's eyes first opened, for a second or more, a frightened stranger had looked out upon a strange room and a strange woman, then, remembering, had wrapped her arms around Theo's neck and held on tight.

As Theo climbed the path up from the beach and topped the rise of the cliff, the wind caught up with her and swirled her hair into her eyes. One cold raindrop plopped against her cheek. Brushing the hair away, she looked out to see Jonathan Tairas walking down from the pools. Mistaking her gesture for a wave, he waved and turned to meet her.

"I've just been talking to the shuttle crew that landed at Base One," he said by way of greeting. "After that I felt the need for fresh air."

"What did they find?"

"It was pretty bad." He took a deep breath.

"What way? What happened?"

"Well . . . Executive Commander Ito is missing. They still haven't found out what happened to him."

"Probably the same thing that happened to the Orlovs," said Theo. "There was simply no witness to his death."

"Probably. Their medical staff believed the fear was mass hysteria and treated the crew accordingly. Five of the medics were killed by enraged patients. What seemed to save the group was an attack by your animals. When that happened, it gave them a common and obvious enemy. They banded together against it. And fear of meeting cave bears kept them from collecting more crystals."

"How many died?"

"Only three."

"Why wouldn't they respond to our calls? Why didn't they ask for help?" said Theo.

"They were afraid. Just as we were afraid to really know what was going on there. And then, of course, some of them are guilty of murder. Most are guilty of mutiny. No one was eager to face the consequences of that."

"What's going to happen to them?"

"Eventually? I don't know. Right now they are under quarantine. As we all are, by the way. The *Vladimir* doesn't want live virus brought aboard. But what was bad about this morning was seeing the people at Base One on screen. You know—" He mentioned a number of names. "You would hardly recognize them. Sunken eyes, severe weight loss, haggard. I wonder if we look as bad?"

Theo was quiet, remembering her shock at Tairas's appearance when he came to fetch her and Karen back from the mountains. As if reading her thoughts, he said, "Yes, I guess we do look—somewhat different."

"I guess we do," Theo said. "But would we be quite human if we did not?"

They walked in comfortable silence, circling the pools, and stood to watch the waterfalls spilling down to the sea. A small flock of kalpas dropped out of the clouds to rest in the nearby treetops. Like great long-legged herons, the creatures swayed and bowed to one another, dancers gone berserk. Dark brown with mad orange eyes, they seemed exotic even for this world. A gust blew and, as if by signal, heads lifted, wings snapped open, and they were airborne, slowly spiraling to enter the clouds again.

"You smile at them with the same pleasure that I smile at a sun storm," Tairas remarked, watching her reaction. "That's what is important, Theo—that joy. Everything else is . . . not incidental, but not as satisfying."

"And subject to change?" suggested the woman. "And therefore dangerous?"

"Yes," he said. "In our position it never pays to be vulnerable."

"Are you gently trying to warn me I may be disappointed?"

"Yes. The Orlovs are an old and wealthy clan. Karen is a result of five hundred years of careful breeding. She is heir to all they were and are—and, I would imagine, to a great deal of what they possess."

"You think Vice Regent Koh will decide to return her to your colony?"

"It would disappoint me if she did. But it would not surprise me. Nor would it be an unjust decision. She has communicated through her first secretary her interest in the joint requests of yourself and Karen. Her staff has apparently spent much time on your biographical files."

"And?"

"She will be here herself tomorrow morning."

XXVIII

THE shuttle was not an elegant craft. Technology dictated its design. It resembled a baking potato with landing gear; dimpled by viewports, knobby with domes. It was impressive for its size in human scale but became insignificant when compared to the smallest parent ship.

Because its weight would sink into the softness of the rain-soaked soil around Base Three, the shuttle landed on a rock shelf some distance away. To the staff watching from camp, the craft appeared as an elongated white ovoid, emblazened with the corporate insignia—an arching aurora. The utility cars were used to taxi the officers down to camp.

To avoid viral contamination, the visitors arrived wearing

isolation gear, much as Theo and Karen had worn in the cave. The garb made them all look the same, one head bubble indistinguishable from the next as they came down the ramp. There was one exception—Vice Regent Koh.

She arrived on the third trip of the taxis, with no fanfare, no ceremony. She needed none. The moment she appeared in the hatchway it was obvious to all onlookers that here was Somebody. Jonathan Tairas came on the run.

Madame Koh was as small as colonials tended to be. To Theo, her face suggested a shrike. Her feathery beige hair, hooded eyes, and ancient, talon-like fingers reinforced the suggestion, as did the way she stood in the hatch, studying those assembled, her helmet turning slowly from left to right and back again.

"Madame. We are honored." Commander Tairas bowed.

"Of course you are, Jon." The reflectors in her helmet obscured her face as she stepped out into daylight. "I thought that was obvious." Theo was unsure from the tone if the remark was intended as humor, but Commander Tairas chuckled.

"Well, what do you think of us?" He gestured toward the staff who stood about. "How do we look?"

"In comparison to Base One personnel—superb. In comparison to the Agricultural Base—superior. But compared to what you looked like when you first arrived, peaked. It is encouraging to see that none of you appears to have gone completely mad. I find that refreshing."

"We have a fine staff," the Commander said. "And, psychologically, I think the natural beauty of the site has been a great advantage."

The shining helmet turned slowly as she viewed the site. "Yes.

You were always impressed by trees, Jon. To me one tree looks very much like the next. Decorative but dull. All this sky, all these living things." The small form shuddered. "Shall we go to the conference room? The sooner I review everything, the sooner I can leave."

As the two of them passed, the Vice Regent slowed and her helmet turned in the direction of Theo and Karen. "Orlov minor?" she asked. The Commander nodded and said something too softly to be overheard. The head bubble turned toward Theo. "Interesting." They entered the hangar.

"How old do you suppose she is?" Karen wondered.

"I have no idea," said Theo. "Why?"

"Much older than she looks?"

"Oh, yes."

"Good. She'll be interested in my meat pudding paper."

"I wouldn't count on it, Karen. She doesn't strike me as being interested in animals."

"Oh, she won't care about the animal part. She will care about what they can do. They can extend their life, time and time again. And we have a big animal who does it, too. I bet she would like to know how."

"So would I," said Theo. "And when we have time . . ." It suddenly dawned on her what Karen was getting at. "You mean she will be interested in it from a totally personal view, as a means to defeat death?"

"Or just to live longer," said Karen. "Plus, what if you could market the process? It would pay back every bit of the money she could lose in this expedition."

There were times, Theo thought as she looked down at Karen,

when the girl seemed years wiser than herself. And a hundred times more shrewd. To Theo cryptobiosis was an interesting phenomenon, but because she had little interest in the unnatural state of human life extended by long periods of nothingness, she had never considered the phenomenon's market potential, which might be considerable. The ultimate pharmaceutical?

"Yes," she said absently. "I suppose it would. But how is this going to help us?"

"It's simple," said Karen. "If the two of us together come up with something this great, not only would it be a shame to separate us—it would be unprofitable."

Theo grinned but shook her head. "All she has to do is put the best biochemists she can buy to work on the problem. Whatever any of us create or discover on an expedition, by the terms of our contract, is the property of the Corporation. Her property. Including specimens."

"Karen Orlov. Karen Orlov. Please report to Conference Room A."

At that announcement Theo felt a cold stab of nerves slice through her self-composure. "Already?" she said. "She couldn't have reviewed anything yet. She's been here only five minutes."

Karen shrugged. "She probably just wants to meet me. I am a relative, after all. And nice, too. Don't worry, Theo."

The fact that she was busy didn't keep Theo from worrying. Among the visitors were fifteen new staff members. Three of them were Theo's responsibility. Depending on the Vice Regent's decision, they would stay, either as permanent staff or to aid the remaining members in packing up and folding camp. Quarters had to be found for them, inoculations given, personal gear stowed, orientation tours conducted, introductions made. She felt it was a credit to her self-discipline that she was able to get them nicely settled in with only ten per cent of her mind functioning on their problems. The rest of her thoughts were reserved for what could possibly be happening with Karen and listening for footsteps running down the hall. Midafternoon came and Karen still had not returned.

"Dr. Leslie. Please report to Conference Room A."

She met Karen coming out of the conference room.

"What happened?"

"Nothing. We've been talking. She asked me questions. Who do I want to live with. What do I want to be. I told her all about my parents. And you. And the cave . . ." Karen shook her head in self-disapproval. "Maybe I talked too much."

"What did she say?"

"Mostly, 'And how do you feel about that?' and 'Interesting.' Go on in. I think she just wants to get to know us both a little."

"What did she think of meat puddings?" Theo asked and then answered in concert with Karen, "Interesting."

XXIX

MADAME Koh sat alone at the head of the table, engrossed in the desk screen. She did not look up as Theo entered and stood hesitantly inside the doorway.

"Please sit down, Dr. Leslie. That can't be comfortable—standing there in awe of me."

Theo sat. In the quiet she could hear faint murmurs from the sound track of the tapes Madame Koh was studying and the sudden brisk rustle of her uniform as she leaned forward to press buttons that rejected old tapes, selected new. As she was still encased in the polarized helmet, it was impossible to tell her reaction to anything. The room smelled faintly of an alien perfume. Theo waited.

Abruptly the lighting went dim. Molecules shifted and the helmet became clear. Theo was now the object of intent study. She returned the interest, stare for stare, for this was a rare animal. And like all animals, it reacted hostilely to being stared at. The hooded eyes narrowed, the too-smooth skin darkened with a flush. The Vice Regent rose, towering at five feet one. Then, as if to deny self-consciousness, she pushed her chair close to the next and sat down again, using the chairs as an impromptu chaise longue. Displacement activity, noted the zoologist in Theo, and felt rather ashamed of herself. "Forgive me for staring. . . ."

"Yes, Dr. Leslie. I am not at ease. It is not my habit to leave the ship. Like a zoo animal, I find a break in routine hard on my nerves." She observed the effect of this confession of vulnerability and, rather surprisingly, smiled. "I see you appreciated that simile. Good. Each small understanding helps. What puzzles me is that I care for your good opinion."

"That is very flattering—"

"I never flatter, Dr. Leslie. I would not demean myself by so common a trick. I have been studying you intently these past several days. Through tapes and official files. I find you quite remarkable. Tell me, for example, how did you endure being alone for a month?"

"Oh, it was no hardship, Madame. I was very happy there. To be where no other human has ever been—"

"You did not find loneliness terrifying?"

Theo was going to explain, then, realizing, said, "We each have our own understanding of loneliness."

The other woman did not reply, but merely nodded assent, then sat seemingly lost in thought. When she spoke again she did not apologize for the long silence.

(169)

"Concerning your petition to adopt Orlov minor. I have made my decision. It is admittedly arbitrary." Theo's breathing became very shallow as she listened.

"The Orlovs are from Palus. But their child has never seen that colony. Because of her family's real estate holdings she holds dual citizenship with Earth. She has never seen Earth. She has never had a home.

"The starship on which she was born is light years away, its crew of strangers scattered now across the galaxy. She may never see either again. Her parents were the one constant in her life. Now they too are gone.

"With their death you entered her life, Theodora Leslie. I am not sure it was an accident." She raised an imperious hand to brush aside any chance that Theo might have the temerity to interrupt. "I know the facts. I saw your tapes. But facts as humans understand them are only part of the pattern—a few scratched tiles of an immense mosaic. You were there for some inexplicable reason, and by that 'fact' became the pole on which this child's world now turns.

"To put it simply, I am afraid that if I separate you two it will destroy Karen. You would go on. You would miss her and worry about her, but I doubt it would inflict lasting damage. But for the child it might be that final tragedy. She might never dare to care about anyone again for fear of losing them. I have seen too many people like that. Emotional cripples. If she was older, of course, she would know loves come and go like those waves down there . . . that none is the last and all are the same."

The too-clear eyes focused on Theo. "You do know that, don't you? You must. You seem quite whole."

"I have not found love so common," Theo said quietly. "And each seems very different to me. Very special."

Madame Koh regarded her, skeptically at first, and then her expression softened. "Perhaps," she said, "and it is not my duty to make you aware of what may be true only for me. As you pointed out before, we each have our own level of understanding."

She swung her feet to the floor and stood up. The interview was obviously at an end. "It pleases me that something good has survived the tragedy and waste of this expedition. And if Orlov minor's"—she glanced at her file—"meat pudding theory is correct, the expedition will not be a financial loss. She may be right. As for the legal details, you will adopt her. The Corporation will continue her financial support as part of her parents' contract. She will retain her own name; her estates are in trust until her majority; she will choose her own course of study. I will suggest you be her Mentor. Her passions appear similar to yours, if inexplicable to me. Possibly due to some old Earth ancestor. Before you go off to find her, page Commander Tairas for me."

"May I thank you?" said Theo. "May I be grateful?"

"No. For in time to come you will no longer be sure whether my decision was based on kindness . . . or on a good sense of what was best for my own interests."

"You underestimate yourself," said Theo, "and you presume where I am concerned. And if you weren't wearing that helmet, I would kiss you."

"And I would never forgive you," said Madame Koh. But she was smiling as Theo left.

(171)

XXX

I T rained less each day the shuttle stayed. With the return of the sun, plants that had sprung up unnoticed in the rain began to bloom. There was a shaggy fringe of flowers around each of the domes where wind-carried seeds had washed down and taken root. Overnight the trees with their seemingly ancient leaves became covered with yellow puffs.

There was little time for the staff to appreciate all this. The Vice Regent kept them busy. Like a house cat, Madame Koh seldom ventured outside. When she did, she could hardly wait to get back in again. She spent her nights aboard the shuttle and her days in Conference Room A. Everyone came to her, and her orders issued forth.

After reviewing the *Vladimir's* medical staff report on the efficacy of Interferon X, she judged the remedy adequate. Theo and Dr. Wexler were commended for their work. Dr. Wexler and Dr. Felix were promptly sent off to the other two bases to administer Interferon X to all staff.

"Orlov minor" and Theo were ordered to complete their preliminary study on meat pudding cells, isolating the control factors in the cryptobiotic process. "I also want a second jointly authored paper on the subject, dealing with your cave bears. Nothing elaborate. An abstract and supporting microscope film will do."

Theo stared at her. The Vice Regent obviously had no idea of the work involved. "But I'm not qualified to—"

"You have three days," Madame Koh told her. "The final pharmaceutical result of this may be very profitable. If so, it will be due to your initial discovery. I want you both legally entitled to share in royalties."

"But what if I'm wrong?"

"What if you're right?"

"But my contract—"

"Will be amended. Do it."

They did it; Karen with great enthusiasm, Theo with mixed feelings. Culture after culture, cell type after cell type, was desiccated, studied, ruined; desiccated, studied, killed—until finally one batch of skin cells revived and split. And told them nothing. Followed by twenty-seven more batches that died. Hour upon hour of tedium to isolate from the nerve tissue of meat puddings a unique molecular chain that served as an activating switch. Its receptor was the crystal virus.

(173)

That discovery made Theo pause and stare for a long time at the computer screen. If the virus infection had continued unchecked, would the result have been cryptobiotic humans? Was the fear and anxiety partially the result of a subtle dehydration? And when the rains ended and the humidity dropped, would humans have begun to wither and dry visibly? All staff members had been infected by the virus. If Interferon X had not been used . . . but it had been.

She did not want to begin to consider the subject truly, but merely made note of it as an avenue for possible future study by biochemical experts. Nor did she suggest its possibilities to Karen.

The cave bear tissue proved easier, since they now had an idea what they were looking for. And it was there—tiny suggestions of immortality among the dendrites. Theo wrote the required abstracts with no confidence and the nagging feeling she might be risking her reputation in a field in which she felt totally unqualified. She could imagine error coming back to haunt her in texts to come. And the scorn of the academics.

"Why do you care?" said Karen. "What you do is alive; what they do is dead. So who cares what they say?"

That such an observation not only made sense to Theo but reassured her made her smile each time she remembered it.

The abstracts were sent in to the Vice Regent. The next morning she sent for Theo.

"We are suspending the Eridan Project," Madame Koh said by way of greeting. "The current staff will leave with the *Prince Vladimir*. It will take quite some time to prepare quarters on the ship and to settle issues here. It is a waste for you to spend that

(174)

now limited time on this planet packing or doing lab work that could be more profitably done aboard ship. I want you and the little Orlov to go back in the field. What is it that makes you smile? That you will leave this world? Or the prospect of being away from my demands?"

"Getting out in the field again. I like this world. If we must leave, it would be a shame to miss seeing its spring. Infants are being born and I don't know how they feed. And where did the cave bears go and how do they reproduce? For they must. And the great swamp creatures . . ."

"Yes." There was no enthusiasm in the word. "While you are out there, for my own curiosity I should like to see pictures of those bear creatures—if you can manage that without becoming lunch. Now, about the Orlovs' grave site. Unless the child objects, we will not disturb it. It seems both morbid and pointless to do otherwise. Do you disagree?"

"No. But I will discuss it with Karen."

"We have your tape of their murder. We have confessions. For those and the others." She noted Theo's questioning look and explained. "I had drugs administered. I made them all relive those days. Interesting."

The little hairs stood up on Theo's arms. As if the staff at Base One were specimens to be studied, she thought, and then in fairness wondered if they were really so different, she and Madame Koh? When presented with inexplicable animal behavior—

"And you will leave by noon," she heard Madame Koh saying.

"I'm sorry. I was thinking of something else."

"Yes. I said I want you away from here, promptly. Not you

particularly, but Orlov minor. Staff from Base One are arriving soon. I am holding the trial here, at this Base. I want the worst of this ugly affair confined to this world. There is a limit to the degree of contamination I will allow aboard the *Vladimir*."

Theo wisely said nothing. Better not to question a statement like that, a power like that. She rose from her seat at the table. "Will we ever come back to Eridan?" she asked.

The Vice Regent was engrossed in something new and answered without looking up. "I won't. You might want to."

XXXI

A N hour later Theo and Karen were high in the air a hundred miles inland. The weather was beautiful. Above them fat clouds drifted south in the sunshine. Below, the formerly arid land shone with rivers and lakes reflecting the sky.

Animals dotted the plains. Every shining water had its complement of wildlife in or around it. All seemed serene and as peaceful as the two of them were beginning to feel. Theo set the speed at observation cruise and they loafed along, sightseeing.

Their conversation consisted mostly of "Look over there!"— at hillsides orange with flowers, at a herd of yellow grazers gamboling with their babies, at an enormous browser mowing its way across a swampy spot, at a rainbow to the north.

Then, "Cave bear!" Karen pointed toward a shallow canyon off to their left. Theo circled down to look. The animal was moving in the curious rippling lope of hexapeds, hurrying toward a small herd of brown grazing creatures who seemed unaware of danger.

When the shadow of the aircraft passed over, the cave bear slowed. Theo circled back and aimed the camera. As it saw the shadow return, the cave bear raised its head and saw the aircraft. If an animal's mouth could be said to drop open in surprise, this one's did. It stopped and stood, staring upward with a bewildered expression. As the craft circled, the cave bear turned also, keeping the aircraft in sight. Then, as if to get a closer view, it climbed the side of the canyon and stood on the highest point to watch them.

"I'll bet it wishes *it* had a camera," said Karen. "Its friends will never believe this story."

"Does give you that feeling, doesn't it?"

"What do you think happens to them?"

"My guess is a few reproduce or breed now. Or both. As their world gets progressively drier, instinct or hormones send them back to their mountain caves to wait for the next rainy season."

"How long do they have to wait?"

Theo shrugged. "Perhaps years. I suspect these creatures are as rare as the rains here. Perhaps the last of their kind. The other animals are not accustomed to being live prey. They have no instinct to flee the cave bears until it's too late. That suggests either unbelievable stupidity—or the simple fact that they are never hunted. I suspect it's the latter."

(178)

"I'd like to see that," said Karen. "Them going back to their caves. The sun setting on a dying species. Make a great space opera—see, these two cave bears fall in love, and one of them dries up for a hundred years and the other gets so lonely—" She saw Theo was giving her "that look" and she subsided into giggles.

"Even Madame Koh should be satisfied with those shots," Theo said. "You see if you can keep the camera on target while we lift away."

"Theo?"

"Yes?"

"Where are we going to camp tonight?"

"Wherever we happen to be that is pleasant."

"Can we go back to your special camp? Would you mind? I know it's spoiled now for you, but . . . I'd like to . . . see how the vots are."

"And say good-bye?"

Karen nodded agreement and concentrated on looking out the window.

"I think the vots spent the rainy season high and dry in their tunnels." Theo spoke to give the girl time to regain her composure. "Vots dig such comfortable burrows. Roomy and well ventilated. They have drying rooms for the hay they cut. And when it's properly aged, they pack it into another chamber for storage. They even have bathrooms that they floor with sand and gravel."

"Do they live together?" Karen sniffed discreetly.

"No. It seems to be one vot per burrow."

(179)

"Don't they get along?"

Theo grinned. "I imagine that if vots see too much of each other it's difficult for them to find new things to talk about."

It was late afternoon when they reached that mountaintop. It could be identified from the air by the spring, a gleaming topaz in the sun's slanting rays. They circled carefully to make sure no cave bears were in the area and then landed above the old campsite.

"Are we on top of vots?" Karen worried.

"No. Solid rock."

As soon as the hatch was open, a breeze drifted in. It smelled sweetly of herbs and drying hay. They got out and stood looking. The rains had made even this place bloom. Grasses grew wherever there was sandy soil. A vine-like plant wreathed over the rocks, decorating them with soft yellow flowers. Swarms of weejees fluttered over those flowers still in sunlight. Theo's cave was deep in grass.

"Vot!" The sound came from somewhere below and echoed and was answered by cohorts. But no vot was in sight. Theo knew from past experience that it would take them a while to get over their shyness.

"I think I'll go down there now," Karen said, pointing to the mound at the edge of the small valley below.

"Shall I come with you?"

"No. I'll go alone." Karen set off down the hill.

While Theo worked, she kept an eye on her. The girl was sitting on a boulder near the mound. She seemed to be talking to the two who slept there. She talked for a long time, long enough for Theo to rig the alarm system carefully above vot height, unroll the sleeping bags, start dinner, and see the sun was beginning to go down.

When she heard footsteps on the rocks, she looked up to see Karen coming back up the path. The girl's eyes were swollen, but she seemed to be at peace with the world. She sat down yoga style on the other side of the cooking area and watched Theo prepare dinner.

"I told them I was footnote stuff now," Karen said after a while. "And I told them all about you. So they would know I was safe. And . . ." She made a desperate little gesture with her hands. ". . . I don't know, Theo, it just doesn't seem fair!"

"Fair has nothing to do with it," Theo said gently but resolutely.

"I know that. Or at least I think I do. But sometimes . . ."

"Yes . . ."

"Vot?"

"I said . . ." Theo started to repeat and then saw Karen beginning to smile. "Look! Up there at the end of the work wagon." The girl pointed.

Theo turned and saw a large vot watching them. It sat with its forepaws folded demurely on its chest. Something small and furry moved behind the landing pods. Up onto the top of a pod hopped a small vot, then another. They stood cheek to cheek and rump to rump and stared at the intruders.

"Baby vots!" Theo was delighted.

"Vot!" said the parent.

"Votlings!" Karen's pitch was loud with inspiration. "Votlings. Baby vots are votlings!"

"Vot?" said the parent.

"Vot! Vot! Vot!" echoed its friends from burrows about.

Theo heard rocks scuffle as Karen moved. She reached out a restraining hand. "I know you want to pick them up," she said softly. "So do I. But we would terrify them. Suppose a vot could pick us up?"

"But they look so cuddly," protested Karen. "And they can't run as fast as the big vots."

"Vot!" echoed the parent and set off another volley. Inspired by this chorus, the infants tried to join in. They stretched their necks and twisted their small, round heads. Their jaws strained with effort. The only sound that resulted was human laughter. As if offended, the parent vot dropped to its paws and disappeared over the rocks. Its children scrambled after.

"We hurt their feelings," Karen said, genuinely contrite. "We did, didn't we?"

"I don't know," came the honest answer. "Perhaps. Or perhaps our laughter is offensive noise to their ears. But they will be back. Vot curiosity outweighs vot dignity. Let's eat our supper."

The three moons rose as they ate. The moonlight gleamed on the spring and cast long shadows between the hills. By its light they could see vots moving about in the night. But nothing else. It was all as peaceful as Theo remembered.

After they climbed into their sleeping bags, the wind died down. In the stillness they could hear the spring splashing down the stones. There was another noise, a brisk snipping sound. "What is that?" Karen whispered. "Vots," Theo whispered back and hoped she wouldn't be overheard by the animals. "They are cutting grass so it will start to dry as soon as the sun comes up."

(182)

"Smart," said Karen. "Theo?"

"Yes?"

"You remember you told me about this being the Inn of the Sky?"

"Yes."

"That's the first thing you told me that I remember." She paused, apparently thinking. "I'll always remember that."

"It's a nice thing to remember," Theo agreed sleepily.

"Because that way, no matter where we go, so long as we can look up and see the stars, we'll be at home there."

Theo smiled to herself in the darkness as she reached over and found Karen's hand. They lay together in companionable silence until sleep came to the inn.

About the Author

H. M. Hoover was born near Alliance, Ohio. She has traveled extensively in the United States and has had ample opportunity to pursue her interests in natural history, history, and archaeology. The author of *Children of Morrow, The Lion's Cub, Treasures of Morrow,* and *The Delikon,* she lives in New York City.